HALLOWS FRIGHT

A HALLOWEEN ROMANCE

NIGHTMARE ACRES

DAKOTA WILDE

HADES PUBLISHING CO., LLC

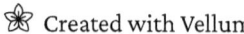

For my spooky babes, gays, and theys.
To the ones who love the dark and creepy things that go bump in the
night, this one is for you.

AUTHOR'S NOTE

Please check the author's website for a comprehensive list of content warnings. This book is intended for a mature audience of 18+ and the subject matter within is not suitable for everyone.

If you find any typos, please email
hadespublishingco@gmail.com

www.dakotawildeauthor.com

CHAPTER 1
OLIVIA

"Boo!" My ex's head appears from behind my front door, causing me to scream.

"God-fucking-dammit, Trent. Why do you have to be such an ass?" My hand is clutched tightly against my chest, trying to quell my racing heart from his jump scare.

"Is that any way to talk in front of the kids?"

Trent always does this. Shows up unannounced and jabbing me with his little judgmental comments, as if he's such a better parent. I stuff any retorts I'd like to say behind my teeth, knowing that little ears are listening to every word we exchange.

Jasmine's small hand pulls at my leg, "Mommy, are you going to let Daddy in?"

Right. I've been too busy grappling with the surprise that is Trent to move away from the door and do the proper thing of letting him in. Even though I don't want to. He still has every right to see our kids. Though, I can't remember the last time he actually made an effort.

"Who wants to go trick or treating?" he bellows, making a scene as he pulls out two brand new princess dresses from behind his back.

The girls screech, jumping up and down as my heart plummets watching this scene unfold.

"Trent, we have plans already," I say in a firm tone, just like the court appointed therapist suggested.

Dealing with a narcissist, you have to approach them differently than you would a normal person. A regular person would understand that swooping in at the last minute can cause a massive disruption, severe disappointment, and even heartbreak. But unfortunately, he just sees it as being spontaneous. He sees it as him being a good dad, and our daughters are the casualties of his behavior. Never mind that I had to beg work for the time off or that I've been looking forward to taking them out all month.

"So, cancel them."

Of course, he would think that weeks of planning their costumes, and painstakingly ordering not one, not two, but three different choices for them because they kept changing their minds on what they wanted to be, was no big deal. His brush off festers under my skin as I watch our girls running off with their new costumes, disappearing down the hall to leave the two of us dangerously alone.

"Trent, their costumes are upstairs, and we have plans to meet up with some other kids in the neighborhood tonight." The effort it takes to be calm while trying to get through to him deserves some sort of medal. Bronze at least.

"Okay, well now they have something they can play dress up in later. Come on Liv, it's not that big of a deal."

And there it is. Confirmation that he doesn't give a shit as usual.

"I wish you would have called first so that I wouldn't have wasted the money." My blood is boiling, and my smile is tight, just like my finances.

"What, so I can't show up and surprise my girls?" he steps closer to me rubbing my forearm, implying that I am still his. He reeks of cheap tobacco and stale beer.

I step back and fold my arms over my chest feeling the ghost of his unwanted touch lingering on my skin. I can't believe I used to allow this man to touch me willingly.

"Oh, okay, whatever. I see how it is. You don't want me to be a father to our girls? I can just leave then." He goes to open the door. I can't tell if he's truly about to leave, or if it's just another one of his manipulations.

"Daddy?" Jasmine reappears wearing a tiara crooked on her short brown curly hair that matches his coloring perfectly, and a glittery dress that isn't pulled on all the way.

My heart twists, wondering how long she's been standing there.

"Daddy's not leaving, right?" I say glaring at Trent, knowing he holds the power to break our little girls' hearts with whatever he decides.

Isobel waddles in, thumb in her mouth and a matching tiara on her head. Her bright blue eyes bouncing between me and Trent.

"Please," I mouth, hoping he won't just take off and crush

our kids' hearts in the process. Knowing him, he's more than capable of it, and it wouldn't be the first time.

"Nah, we're going trick or treating! Grab your bags, munchkins, and let's go." He says after far too long of a pause.

I exhale as they take off running again.

"She's still sucking her thumb?" He frowns as he rubs his unshaven face. I used to find it attractive, but now he just looks sloppy. He's let his brown hair grow out to try and cover the bald spot that's forming on the crown of his head, but it's still clear there's one there. He crosses his arms and fixes me with a stern judgmental glare, eyebrows raised as he waits for my answer.

"Yeah," I say tightly, crossing my arms as well.

"Well, what are you going to do about that?"

I close my eyes, not wanting to rise to the bait. The tension is palpable throughout my entire body, his presence enacting a response in me that has me feeling immediately on the defense. Truthfully, I want to scream at him and unleash every repressed thought, list every transgression, every hurt, every piece he broke in me. But I know it won't do any good.

Trent always has an excuse. A way to twist things around and make it seem like he has no responsibility for the things he's done. Or worse, gaslight me into wondering if what I experienced with him is what really happened.

And tonight, I don't have the fight in me. I just paid off Isobel's doctor's bill from when she got strep at the beginning of the month. It was enough to have me eating bread sandwiches for the last few weeks so the girls wouldn't suffer.

"I'm ready, Daddy. Coming, Mama?" Jasmine asks holding

her trick or treat bag in one hand, and her sister's arm in the other.

They look adorable, and I wonder how they got so big so fast.

"Nah, Mom's going to stay here. I'll have them back in the morning." Trent answers before I can say anything.

Tears sting in my eyes as my mouth opens and closes, wondering what to say or do.

"You know what, you guys have fun with Daddy, and I'll see you tomorrow," I force out with a wobbly smile.

I know what our custody agreement says, and even if I were to put up a fight, it would cause the girls to miss out on Halloween, and the police hate getting involved. We've been down that road before and they didn't do anything but shrug their shoulders and scold us to get along.

"Let me get a picture first before you go," I say pulling out my phone.

Immediately, the girls strike a pose puckering their little lips and flashing a peace sign. I take several pictures from different angles, and each photo I take, they do a little change in their pose. "Okay, last one but just of you guys smiling." They give me a crazy, William Dafoe like grin and I can't help but laugh at their antics.

"I'll have them back by eleven tomorrow morning," Trent says, walking out the door with the girls in tow.

As the door closes behind them, I feel a piece of my heart go with. Wishing, not for the first time, that things could be different.

"He did what?" My best friend, Callie, screeches in my ear. She's no stranger to Trent and how unreasonable and downright cruel he can be. Having been my support system through the many, many court dates while we finalized our divorce and child custody arrangement, she saw first-hand just what he was capable of.

"I know. But the worst part was when he tried to call me one of his girls." His touch still lingers on my skin, and not in a good way.

"Ugh. That's it. Get your ass ready, right now. We are going out." Typical Callie, always bossing me about.

"Where?"

"No questions, just get ready."

I'm met with a loud dial tone in my earbuds as she leaves me wondering what she has cooked up at the last minute. Leave it to Callie, to find something though. We've been best friends since kindergarten. Always there for each other in the good times and the bad. And for the last two years, I've been using that best friend punch card a whole hell of a lot. I owe it to her to clean myself up and have a night out, like old times. Even if she is a little harsh sometimes, she's still my best friend.

It's been such a long time since I put on makeup and curled my hair for myself, that I'm taking my time and using my best products. I put on a playlist to help distract me from the sad state my life has turned into, dancing along to Chappell Roan at full blast. I let the upbeat notes of *Pink Pony Club* flitter away at my bad mood, letting my hips wiggle along to the beat while I sing off-key. The light above my bathroom sink flickers, reminding me that I need to change it out, but I haven't had time.

I add it to the internal, never-ending list of things I have to do.

Shaking my hips while I apply my foundation, I realize it's a shade too dark. But I think I can make it work. I just need to blend the shit out of it and hope my concealer works its magic. In this lighting, it seems to be doing just that. Hopefully, wherever we're going it isn't too bright. At least it's covering up the few stress induced pimples that dot my chin.

My thoughts drift to the girls, hoping they're having a good time. Knowing Trent, they're being treated to a good time, only it's the after part that worries me. He's good at showing off, making them laugh, but then as soon as morning comes, the magic spell wears showing his true nature. I wonder just how long it will be until he comes back around again after this. He doesn't see how much the girls miss him. Always asking when Daddy will be back, and I never have an answer for them. I get to watch firsthand as he breaks their hearts with nothing I can do to legally stop it from happening.

"Knock, knock, bitch. I hope you're dressed." Callie's voice echoes off the tiles of my bathroom. I love that we have the kind of relationship where she can let herself in.

"Don't act like you haven't seen it all before." I roll my eyes, putting on some lip-gloss in a deep berry shade that gives the right finishing touch I was hoping for. Looking in the mirror, I see my blonde hair tumbling over my shoulders in beachy waves. My green eyes are framed by black long lashes that I've curled and applied one too many coats of mascara onto. But, I have to admit I look fucking good. A whisper of the girl I was before Trent got his claws into me. I missed this girl, well, woman. I am in my early thirties.

"Damn, you look good. All this for little old me?"

"So do you, babe. Are you going to tell me where we're going?"

"Not a chance, but you should wear flats."

Interest piqued, I rifle through my closet and settle on a pair of old Vans to go with my black leggings and grey *Sleep-token* hoodie.

"I hope you don't mind, but I invited Shayla and her fiancée, Penny. I know Shayla can be a little much, but it's just for one night."

"Nah, that's fine. I was a last-minute addition anyway." I've known Shayla for as long as I've known Callie with them being sisters it's hard to avoid ending up together. Truthfully, her boisterous personality gets under Callie's skin more than it does mine. I find her hilarious and enjoy seeing her make Callie squirm as only sisters can.

"Bitch, you're always first in my book," Callie says, linking her arm in mine as we head down the narrow staircase. We barely fit, but that just makes us giggle. Her long black hair sways behind her. It's so long that it brushes against the top of her non-existent ass.

"Are you two already starting with your shit?" Shayla calls up as we round the staircase landing.

"Are you already complaining?" Callie quips, and I elbow her.

She glares at me and then relents. "Fine. Let's get going. We don't want to be late."

"For what?" I ask, grabbing my purse and keys.

"You'll see."

Whatever it is, it has to beat staying home and sulking. So, I follow. Locking the door firmly behind me.

CHAPTER 2
OLIVIA

We drive down a secluded path tucked away in the middle of nowhere. The pines press in from all around us as several flickering torches light the way. It's unsettling, but also entrancing how ethereal it all looks. Enveloping us into its warm embrace. A fine layer of fog rolls along the ground, kicking up into circles as we pass through it. I still have no idea where we're headed, but seeing this has me feeling nervous.

"Are you sure this is the right place?" Shayla snaps at Callie from the back.

"For the last time, yes. I followed the directions."

"Still, it's crazy it doesn't show up on GPS at all. Shouldn't businesses list their locations on the map?" Shayla utters.

"Whatever. Maybe they're a little more old school. I, for one, like the nostalgia. Don't you remember having to print out directions when we were little for mom?"

"Wait. What the hell is that?" Penny asks, and we all look in the direction that she's pointing. Callie slows the car down to a crawl as we peer into the dark. Deep in the trees, there's what looks like gallows, with several hanging bodies swinging back and forth. Only, there's no breeze tonight.

"Creepy. Those videos on TikTok saying this place is the most life-like they've seen, might not be wrong." Shayla mutters.

"I told you. This place is worth it." Callie quips, pressing on the gas.

The word, 'lifelike', spins in my head, fearful of what that means. I've always hated haunted houses, choosing instead to attend more festivals and play dress up. I leave the scarier elements of this holiday to Callie, who seems hellbent on us dragging us along to whatever this place is. Wherever we're going seems creepy as fuck.

We come to a fork in the road where, a large ten-foot-tall statue of a pumpkin headed man waving. His skeletal arm points us to the right as he holds a sign in the other arm that reads, "This way to your doom".

Unease coats my stomach, but Callie turns the car in that direction completely unaffected. As we turn, a sign with two jack o'lanterns on either end flickers a chilling welcome to Nightmare Acres. The jagged letters look as if they're about to fall off at any moment to smash us as we pass below.

"What is this place?" I ask.

"Babes, it literally says on the sign, Nightmare Acres." Callie replies, and I bristle at her response. "There's a corn maze, a haunted house, a haunted hayride, and in the summer, they have a week-long camp where they chase you night and day."

My eyebrows raise. "Sounds intense." Suddenly, I'm not so

sure this is a good idea. I wanted to get out of the house for once, but there's something in the air here that has me on edge. I grip the seatbelt, wishing I could just turn back around.

The car comes to a stop in a packed gravel parking lot. In the distance, a lone building flashes with an ominous red glow. Its several stories high, looming around the surrounding area.

"Looks like someone is trying to compensate for something." Shayla murmurs, snaking Penny's hand in hers. They spent the majority of the time on the drive over making out with each other, and God, it made me jealous. I don't begrudge them their happiness, but seeing them so in love only reminds me of how alone I've been. The last person I kissed was Trent.

That depressing bit of knowledge clings to my skin as we exit the car and are met with the smell of beer and hay.

"Ladies, right this way!" Shayla shouts, leading the way to where a line has formed around the tall building.

Looking up at the imposing structure, I determine it has to be at least five stories high.

Five stories of pure torture.

The area is teeming with people in all sorts of costumes, some coming right up and staring eerily at us as we pass. Some jumping out of the dark shadows, and we aren't even at the entrance yet.

There's a crowd gathered around a masked man, abs on display as he arches his back, bellowing a flame out of his mouth. The crowd gapes and claps as he takes a deep bow, eyes finding mine. I look away quickly, but can't shake the feeling that he's still staring.

Sure enough, when I turn to look back, he's standing, eyes glued to my direction.

Callie knocks into me. "Oh fuck, he's hot."

I nod my head in agreement, following her lead. As crazy as it feels to admit, seeing the way he looked at me ignited something in me. Something that feels akin to desire.

A few people stumble out of the exit wearing matching "I survived Nightmare Acres" t-shirts looking like they fully enjoyed themselves, but the splatters of fake blood on their faces and arms give me pause.

"You're not chickening out on me, are you?" Callie asks, breaking me from my slight panic.

I know if I tell her I'm out, she'll respect my decision. But all that waits for me at home is watered down wine, an empty bed, and a head full of regrets, so I decide to vagina up and go in.

"Nah, I'll stay."

"That's my favorite bitch. We're going to have fun, you'll see. I was here last weekend."

"With Janna?"

She wiggles her eyebrows at me. "Mayyybeee."

"Well, I want to hear all about it. Did she ask you out or did you ask her?"

"I asked, and we're keeping it casual for now."

"For now? That's promising."

Callie is extremely averse to having a committed relationship. We joke that we are each other's longest relationship, because in a way it's true.

We wait in line as distant screams penetrate through the walls. Thankfully, it's not too cold of a night. Some years before, it snowed on Halloween when Jasmine was barely one years old, making trick or treating absolutely miserable. My mind slips to wondering if the girls are having a good time with Trent.

Maybe I should text them.

I worry my bottom lip, already piecing together the kind of response that would get from my ex. Knowing him, he'd take out his frustration on the girls. It's best just to wait out the night, even though it kills me.

"Hey. They're fine," Callie says, bumping my hip with hers, knowing exactly what I'm thinking of.

"It's just hard to leave them. Especially with Trent. You remember that time he lost Isobel at Summer Fest?"

She nods. "I lost my good flip flops looking for her."

I breathe out of my nose, remembering the fear I felt that day. Of course, the judge presiding over our case just shrugged his shoulders and said, "It happens. Young kids take off all the time."

He didn't care to hear that he lost her because Trent had been too busy hitting on one of the carnie workers. I groan into my hands.

"They'll be fine, Olivia. He most likely learned his lesson."

"Most likely. Now I feel better."

She gives me a sad smile and tucks me against her for a quick hug, arms sliding around my tense shoulders. She knows that because of our court ordered agreement, I have no choice but to let my girls go with him.

"Let's try to enjoy the night together, yeah?" Her eyes plead with me, and I relent, forcing myself to take in my surroundings and be present.

A man on stilts walks past leaning down every once in awhile to make faces at people who aren't paying attention.

When they finally notice he's there, they scream and then laugh, as he moves on to his next target. A few take some selfies with him to post on their socials.

I'm too engrossed in what he's doing, that I don't notice the menacing presence right behind me.

It starts as a low growl, making the hair on the back of neck stand on end. Eyes wide, I whip around finding nothing but air. That was fucking creepy, I think as I scan the line.

Unease fills my stomach as we inch closer to the ticketing counter. Maybe I'm just imagining things.

"Step right up, have your ID's ready." A man dressed as a creepy marionette, with strings attached to the ceiling calls out. Another man with a bushy mustache, a bright red clown nose, and a scar slashed across his face presents us with a waiver.

"Sign here."

My eyes flick over the terms, seeing a lot of standard contract language, that is until I land on one glaring word. "Death?" I shriek.

"They have to say that to cover their asses." Callie says, signing her form and handing it back, popping her gum. "Come on. It'll be fun." The man checks her ID, and hands it back with an evil cackle that sends a shiver up my spine.

Shayla and Penny hand their forms in, but mine is still clutched tightly in my hands. Tight enough to wrinkle the offensive paper. Surely, no one has died here, right?

Maybe it's just for people with health conditions, and it's covering their ass like Callie said.

Nibbling on my bottom lip while I debate, the marionette crouches down until he's level with my face. "In or out, sweetheart. We've got a line full of people *dying* to get in." His breath smells like cigarettes, and has my nose wrinkling, taking a half step back.

"Fuck it." I sign my name and hand both my ID and the paper to the mustache man.

He grins, looking down at my ID. As he hands it back to me, his leathery hand brushes against mine and a ticket to Nightmare Acres is folded into my palm . "Have fun, *Olivia*." His deep, sinister voice growls just low enough for me to hear.

Shit.

Why do I get the feeling that I'm going to regret this later?

CHAPTER 3

PHANTOM

Another Halloween is in full swing, and I'm living for it. Well, living might be a stretch since I'm dead and all. A fucking phantom only here to instill fear and get my kicks from making the living scream bloody murder. It gives my long dead heart a jolt, tethering me to this plane of existence. The crowd's energy is extra palpable with it being Halloween. My spirit is stronger. Hungrier. Practically salivating at the morsels of fresh meat traipsing around our hallowed grounds in their various costumes. Pretending to be what we really are— monsters.

I'm craving something sweet tonight, and I think I found the perfect little snack. Her blonde curled hair tumbles down her back and her black leggings hug her every curve, making me want to sink my teeth into that tight ass of hers. I bet she screams so pretty.

Sniffing the air, her warm cashmere and cinnamon scent calls to my more base instincts. It's intoxicating and inviting.

I can barely contain my growl as I pass her in the line waiting to get into our playground. This place houses many lost souls, both alive and dead. All enacting on our monstrous desires and reaping the rewards.

Nightmare Acres is for the dark, the depraved, and the lost.

This girl definitely fits the bill for being the latter. It practically clings to her— how out of place she feels. From my vantage point above, I can take her in without letting her know I'm here watching. Studying. Planning on how I can get her alone.

"What do you think, Matchbox?" I ask my demonic friend who has a penchant for playing with fire. None of us, except for Talon, can remember our real names. So we picked ones that fit our personalities. He fiddles expertly with the lighter, wielding the flames along his fingertips. The light gleams off his golden horns.

"I think tonight tops last year's Halloween by a mile." He muses. A distant shriek of terror calls out before being suddenly silenced and a knowing smirk takes over my lips.

Word of mouth is a powerful tool, drawing people to our patch of paradise for them to revel in the darkness. Some never stop, joining our forces or ending up six feet beneath us. It just depends on how fucked up their souls are.

The evil ones rot.

The pure ones escape.

And the twisted, well... the twisted tend to join our ranks or just keep coming back for more.

An itch deep in my soul yearns to be scratched, and I think this vixen of a woman is just the right one for the job.

Jumping down from my perch, I find my prey in the sea of souls just dying to get inside our gates.

I follow closely behind as her friend group is enveloped by the darkness. The cackle of crones in the first room they pass, sends a shiver even down my spine. Those witches are hell on earth and not to be trifled with. Their spells entrance and mystify, making the guests sluggish and pliable, opening their minds up just enough for us to fuck with them. That's why everyone who enters comes through here first.

Watching from the shadows, I see the first crone cast her spell over the group she's with. They circle the friends hands grasped tightly as they begin to chant. It's been awhile since I've seen their work, and it's truly something to behold. Impressive, and demanding of my respect. All of us are equipped with our own talents. The witches have their spells, the demons can snatch souls, the vampires can manipulate, the clowns... actually, I'm not sure what the fuck the clowns do other than be fucking creeps. But the ghosts, we can become corporeal, causing things to move without being seen, bending reality at will. Or sometimes, if we wish to be seen, that can be arranged, as well.

"What are you doing down here, ghosty? Don't you have your own section to stick to?" One of the crones asks as I pass through.

"Found something enticing." I nod at the group heading up the stairs to the left, running my tongue over my teeth.

"You know he doesn't like it when we break the rules, Phantom."

"I don't give a shit. I've done more for this place than

most." I quip, ducking past her to follow the object of my desire and out of the path of the next group being let in.

No one likes to feel stuck. Chained to this small plot of land until the end of time. Or until our contract ends. Whichever comes first. With the way humans are speeding up global warming, it might not be that much longer, honestly. Regardless, I want to enjoy whatever time I have left on this plane starting with her.

I don't know what it is that calls to me. Something more than just her scent and sweet, fuckable ass. Something deeper that has me ascending the rickety stairs and braving the florescent strobe lights. It has me following that curiosity, maybe to my own detriment, but I don't fucking care. I'm entranced.

Hot on her heels, if I wait for the right moment, I can get her alone and right where I want her. Thankfully, I know this place like the back of my hand. The rooms are a labyrinth of terror, each unveiling a new horror. Carefully crafted frights and delights that draws people in from all over. A Venus flytrap disguised as an innocent Halloween past time. Though, the rooms consistently move, they're like a clock. Turning like a dial, unseen to the human eye, but felt by us monsters.

It's pure genius really. The creatures of the night all being able to gather in a place where humans think they're interacting with costumes. Not seeing us for what we truly are until it's too late.

Blending in against the walls, I catch up to where she's gripping her nails into the arm of her friend. Blonde hair reflecting the blood red lights strobing from above. Like a warning sign that I should stop, but I've never been one for listening.

A deranged scream slices through the room as a woman with crooked pigtails and fake blood smeared across her low-cut surgeon's outfit wields a plastic axe through the air, chopping at the group. It's clear she's one of the mortal actors they hired. The group of friends break apart, running to dodge the actor's wide reach. Perfect, I smirk. Without her friends to cling to, I can corral her into my domain.

She covers her face screaming as the girl chases her into a corner, tilting her head menacingly. "Scared, bitch?" She trails the tip of the axe against my girl's neck and the fear emanating from the corner she's in is palpable.

A feeling like a mixture of anger and possessiveness rears up in my chest, and I find myself emerging from the shadows and becoming corporeal, grabbing onto the shoulder of the axe wielding actor.

"I wouldn't do that if I were you."

The girl turns, taking me in. It's unclear in this lighting if she recognizes who I am or not, but I don't fucking care. I push her against the wall with my arm against her throat. "Don't fucking touch her again, or next time, that axe will be lodged in your chest." I warn.

My girl stares at us open mouthed. Eyes wide and bouncing between myself and the axe wielding psycho.

"Th-thanks," my girl manages to say, peeling herself off the wall, then looking around as if trying to find where her friends have gone. If I had to guess, they're long gone into the maze by now.

"You can follow me if you want," I offer, trying to act as if being next to her isn't the whole reason I abandoned my post. She nods. "But keep close. You never know what's hiding in the shadows here." I tug her against my side and feel the way she fits perfectly against me. If she only knew what I am. Would she scream in fear? Run for me so I could give chase.

Fuck, the thought of her running from me gets my cock all hard.

I smirk, laughing to myself that she trusts me so freely, following me deeper into my dark playground, and right into my trap.

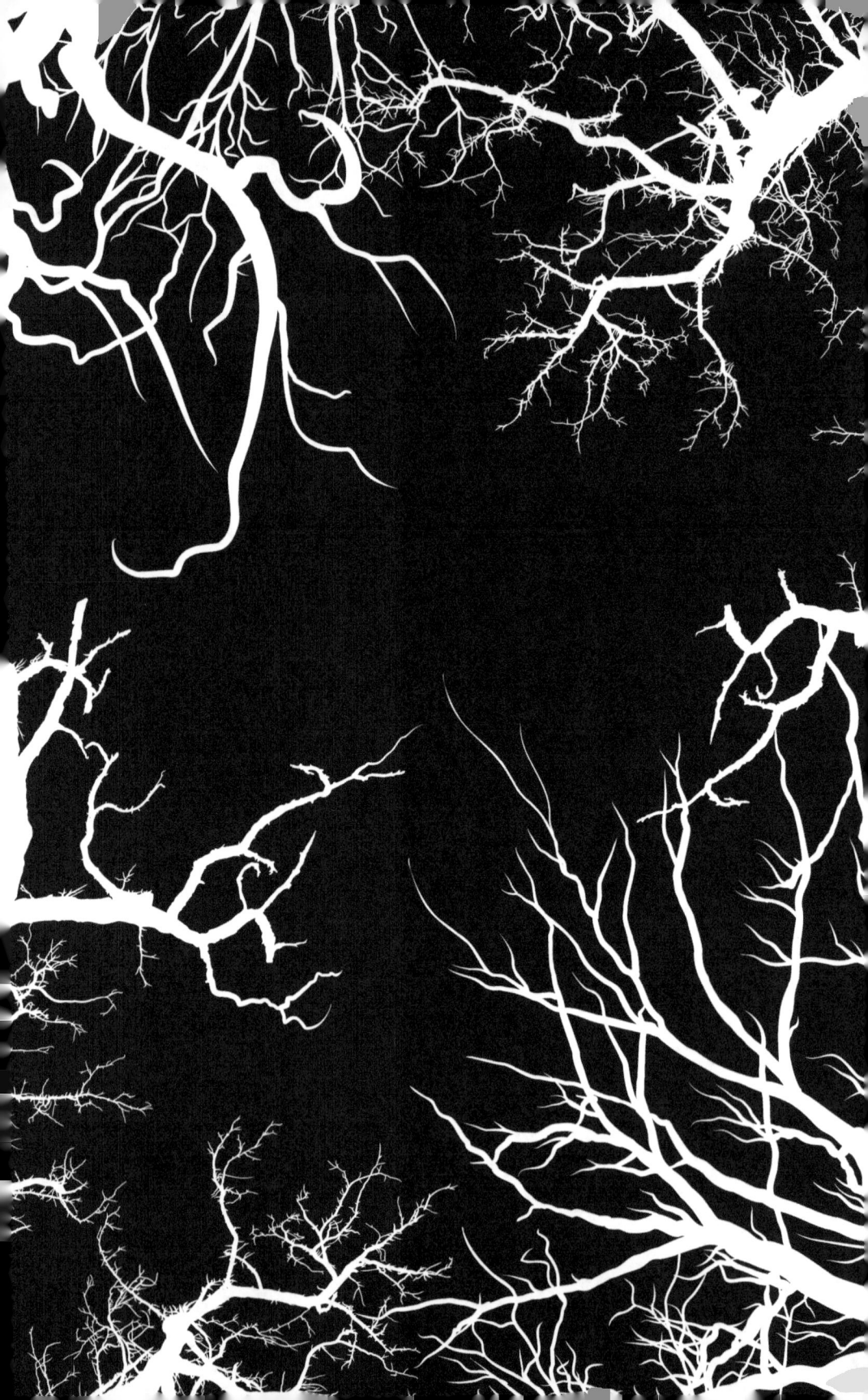

CHAPTER 4
OLIVIA

Nightmare Acres is the perfect name for this house of horrors. Even though, I've only been through a few rooms, it feels like it goes on forever. Never knowing what lays behind the corner or what fresh hell I'll be scared with next. I have no idea where my group is, and now I'm being led by the hand by this admittedly hot as fuck stranger. His hand is firm and calloused against my smaller one, but it's cold, like he spent too long outside in the line. I'm surprised I didn't see him while I was out there. I feel like I would remember him because he's incredibly hard to miss. He has to be at least 6 foot 3. And those broad shoulders make me want to dance my fingertips along them. All dark hair and brooding eyes. A jawline that could cut glass. For the strangest reason, I find myself wanting to lick it. Maybe even nibble down his stubble clad neck a little too.

Fuck, Olivia. You need to calm down, girl. I mean it has been a long time since I've been with anyone. The last time was... was it really when I got pregnant with Isobel? It has to be.

That's just sad.

Maybe letting loose with a stranger is just what I need. And I know Callie would be encouraging the shit out of me to let my inner slut out to play. That part of me has been buried and shut down for such a long time.

The walls around us feel distorted and my vision wobbles with each pulse of the lights. Everything moves around me as I follow this hot stranger deeper into the haunted house. A scream comes from the room we're headed into and my heart races, preparing myself for the worst.

As if on cue, someone dressed as a bloody butcher wielding a cleaver jumps out at us, causing us to step back. I cling to my perfect stranger burying my face in his well-worn leather jacket.

He wraps his arm around me, pulling me around and into his chest. My fingers find his jacket collar, while my adrenaline pumps feverishly through my veins. The fake blood scent permeates the air around us, but in this moment with him clutching me tightly, everything around us seems to melt away. I forget where we are both in time and space. Nothing exists except me and him. This stranger feels like my salvation when I've known nothing but heartache and struggle for years.

I watch, hypnotized as he licks his lips slowly.

Seductively.

Maybe it's the adrenaline or the way that I haven't slept with anyone in years, or maybe it's the way this man looks at me like he wants to steal my soul, but I find myself leaning into him. Moving closer to him as he leans down.

"Ahhhh!"

We break apart, heart racing at a group of people pushing their way in screaming while being chased by the bloody butcher. He pulls my wrist and we're off running again through the maze of rooms. This time we end up in a room that seems to press in on us as we squeeze through. The ceiling dips and walls shrink together,

"Crawl, you fucking pigs!"

A disembodied voice crackles through what appears to be coming from every direction. It's just a sound system, I tell myself, though the way the voice traveled across my skin felt so fucking real.

The stranger crawls through the space first, and I follow, dropping to the ground, grateful for my leggings.

The floor feels disgustingly sticky against my palms as we crawl deeper, the lights getting dimmer as we go until it's completely pitch black.

My fingers graze against something stringy dangling down. Without being able to see what it is, my brain goes wild, imagining all the things it could be. Spiderwebs? Please, don't let it be spiderwebs.

More and more strings come as I push forward. It touches my hair, my neck, sliding over my shoulders. My face gets caught in one and I let out a scream, trying to back up, swatting at where I think the thing is only to meet nothing but air.

I don't know why I let Callie talk me into this. My skin is crawling, and I feel the need to get out, out, out.

"This way," the stranger calls out, and I go, crawling as fast as I can until a bright light emerges and I tumble down into a pit of blood red balls. The walls are moving with a projection of

29

spiders crawling up and down them. Bodies wrapped in spider-webs writhe. Their screams are muffled, and I remind myself again that this isn't real.

Swatting at my own face, I try to get the feeling of the strings off me.

He pulls a white spiderweb from my hair and I can feel my bottom lip quivering from having an overwhelm of emotions.

My friends are nowhere to be found, my kids are out with their dead-beat dad doing god knows what, and now I'm trapped in this haunted house with a guy who's name I don't even know.

He wipes a stray tear from my eyes looking down at me with such intensity I can feel it all the way to my toes. Lights flash around the room, making it seem like he's moving in slow motion as he leans in close, pushing me against the wall of the ball pit. "Don't be scared." He whispers before closing his mouth over mine.

I let him kiss me, leaning into his hard chest and wrapping my arms around his neck. My fingers find his hair and I pull a little on the short strands as he ravages my mouth. His tongue slides against mine and I welcome it. Tasting him sends a jolt of heat down into my core. I feel alive. Every bit of my body craves to be touched, to be taken by him and that scares me.

My pulse rushes and I lose all sense of time. His hands roam up my body and I arch into him. Wanting him to feel me.

"I can't wait to savor all you have to give," he says breaking apart our kiss and working his cool lips up my neck.

"I don't even know your name." I whisper back biting down on his bottom lip as he wraps his hands into my hair deepening our kiss.

"Get back to work!" A voice booms overhead and he pulls back suddenly, chuckling darkly. He places a finger over my lips. "Run. I'll come and find you." He instructs with another kiss.

When my eyes flutter open, he's gone and I'm alone in the room with nothing but the animatronics. flashing lights and an eerie feeling that I'm being watched.

"Run!" his voice calls again, but I have no idea where it's coming from.

Goosebumps erupt on my skin, my heart racing with an ominous sensation that something dangerous is looming close by. I don't hesitate to get the fuck out of here and take off into the next room at full speed.

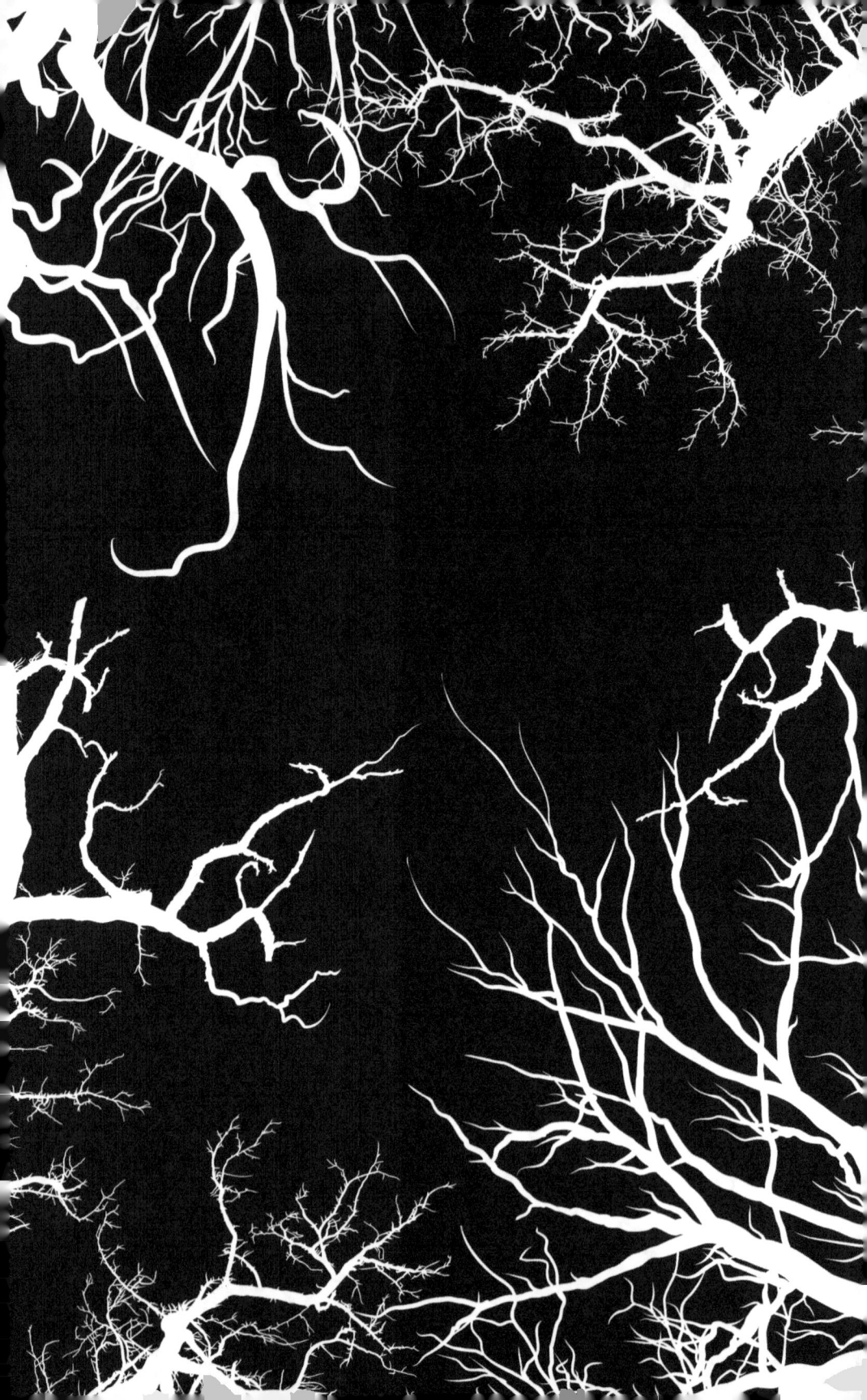

CHAPTER 5
PHANTOM

Maybe it's wrong to trick her into thinking I'm a regular person and not a fucking ghost, but it allows me to be close to her. And fuck, those lips of hers are downright sinful. I can't help but imagine those plush, wet beautiful things wrapped around my cock. I bet she can take it all the way to the back of her throat.

There's five rooms between the one she's in now, and the one I'm tasked to haunt by my boss.

Normally, I wouldn't try and cross Talon and his rules, but there's just something irresistible about this girl that has me willing to break them.

Unlike me, Talon is a human turned vampire. And he has the temperament of an evil dictator. Running this place like his own personal kingdom.

There's a hierarchy of sorts that he enforces. Vampires on the top tier, and no surprise ghosts and poltergeists are on the bottom.

"Where the fuck have you been?" Matchbox asks. "I've had to cover for you. Told them you were out checking the perimeter."

"Thanks man." I see he's changed into the *Ghostface* costume, hiding his black horns from view.

"Whatever. You know I've got your back no matter what. Let's just hope Talon doesn't find out."

"I think if he doesn't already, he will soon. The watcher interrupted a hell of a good kiss." I ache to get back to her, and feel those sinful lips against mine again.

"That's what you were doing? If you weren't already dead, I'd think you had a death wish. You know how he feels about fraternizing with the patrons."

"So, it's okay to kill them, but making out with them is a step too far?" I scoff.

"I don't make the rules, man."

We get in position as we're alerted to another group about to enter our domain.

Digging deep, I unleash my inner monster. Becoming the ghost. A whisp of terror to torment and haunt. Letting a cruel laugh out of my mouth, it echoes around us, bouncing off the pitch-black walls. Following the couple closely behind, I pull the girl's braid and she shrieks, trying to move closer to her boyfriend. But he's too busy being picked off the floor by Matchbox.

"What the fuck?!" he cries, feet kicking at the air. The dude is a complete douche, I can tell. Backwards baseball cap and a heart full of hate, I can taste the sour air around his corrupt soul. The monstrous bloodlust that lives in my veins is just begging to be set free, to consume his darkness.

I know that if I let him walk away from this place, he'll do more harm than good, as evidenced by the yellowing bruises that trail up his girlfriend's arms and the one on her face that she tried to cover with makeup.

Not an ounce of remorse fills me as I suck out his soul, leaving him as a lifeless husk of flesh on the floor. The soul thrashes about for a moment, screaming in agony as it's absorbed into me. It feels so fucking good. Like a high I could never achieve when I was alive.

The girlfriend is long gone, rushing off into the void, and hopefully onto a better life without this piece of shit to abuse her.

"You could have at least left me some." Matchbox complains.

"I'm sure there's plenty more on their way. This town seems riddled with his kind."

He just nods, rolling the lifeless body into position while I press a hidden button on the wall, revealing a trap door that opens easily for us to shove him into. That last body should meet our quota for the year. This season has been busy and with the heightened tourism thanks to some viral videos, it's allowed us to feast regularly.

The vampires should be satiated at least until the summer season, if not longer with how much fresh blood they've gorged themselves on.

Plans for the campers to spend a whole week here are well under way, and I've been finding myself excited at the prospect of chasing fresh meat with no time limits. All day. All night. Just pure terror whenever we feel like it.

"Phantom." The Watcher's voice crackles from the speaker above.

"Fuck." Dread coils in my stomach. I knew it was a risk going after the girl like I did, but it was so fucking worth it. The taste her on my tongue lingers still, taunting me to finish what I started with her. Knowing she's running around, terrified, alone and vulnerable makes me want to abandon my post all over again.

"Get your ass in the office. Now," the Watcher demands and I know I'm truly fucked.

"You rang?" I ask, popping my head into Talon's office. Or rather, lair. Its decor looks like it's been directly transported from Transylvania, complete with high arch ceilings and gothic sculptures. Several gargoyles are affixed to the black and crimson covered walls. Candles flicker and dance creating long ominous shadows about the darkened room.Talon likes to keep reminders of the past while forced to live in the modern age. I'd say he's adapted quite well for himself seeing as he's the creator and owner of this depraved place.

In the corner of the room sits what can only be described as a wall of screens. It shows countless groups of people being scared, attacked, or murdered from every angle of the compound. A gorgeous sight.

"What the hell kind of game are you playing at out there?" he asks, security footage pulled up on one of his many monitors. Showing a zoomed in portion where I'm kissing the hell out of my girl.

"Nothing," I shrug, trying and failing to appear nonchalant.

He turns to face me, fangs on full display, black wavy hair slicked back with a streak of gray on his right side over his ear, and a finely tailored suit hung about his tall frame. "Nothing, my ass. You've abandoned your post for some hot piece of ass. And if anyone is going to be getting that, it's going to be me. Understand?"

I crack my knuckles, knowing that one wrong word and he'll throw me out of here. Or worse, have my contract terminated. And then it's a one-way trip back to the pit of Hell.

Talon is centuries old and one of the most blood-thirsty, murderous vampires alive. But with modern technology, mortals slowly began to catch onto his penchant for killing. To go undetected, he started Nightmare Acres. A place for the creatures of the night to quell our monstrous desires, but only in service to him.

Contracts were signed and too many of us didn't read the fine print. Myself included. But I don't mind the servitude. It's a chance to live.

"You know the rules, Phantom." I look up at the black ceiling. "No leaving your post without approval."

I roll my neck and look him in his ice-cool grey eyes. I know that look well and smirk. He's intrigued. I don't blame him. My girl has something that calls to my inner beast, and obviously I'm not the only one feeling it.

"I don't recall giving you permission." Talon's demeanor is deadly as he flicks his tongue over his sharpened canines. It's almost unfair how otherworldly and seductive the vampires look. As if they've been sculpted to purposefully lure us under their captivating beauty. "Do you remember me giving you permission?"

"No."

He stands to his full height, a whole five inches taller than when he was alive. "No?"

In a blink he goes from the other end of the room to inches away from my face. Using his vampire speed to intimidate me. His form towers over me and his musky scent fills the air. I'm so close, I could lick his Adam's Apple.

"No, sir."

His finger traces my jawline, reaching through the planes of existence to where my solid form resides, and touches my skin. "If you want to play with this human, you'll be playing with me, or not at all." His hand moves down my body and cups my semi-hard cock. "Do you want to play, Phantom?"

I'm well aware of Talon's reputation, but the temptation for a little fun is too much to pass up.

"Where is she now?" I ask, and he smirks, stroking my length into a full hard on. I thrust into his hand, letting him feel how big and ready I am.

"The church." His tongue licks across my bottom lip, canines digging in. A drop of blood coats his teeth and his dark eyelashes flutter closed as he tastes me.

"Do we have a deal?" he asks, still working my dick. His hard cock presses against my lower belly. The scent of arousal lingers between us as we strike a deal to hunt for our precious prey, together.

"Deal. Once we find her, we share her," I agree and feel the deal we've made slide into place.

"Let's go capture our little ghoul," he says, backing away and shifting before my eyes into his bat form.

A distant howl rips through the room as we set into the night to stalk our prey. Together.

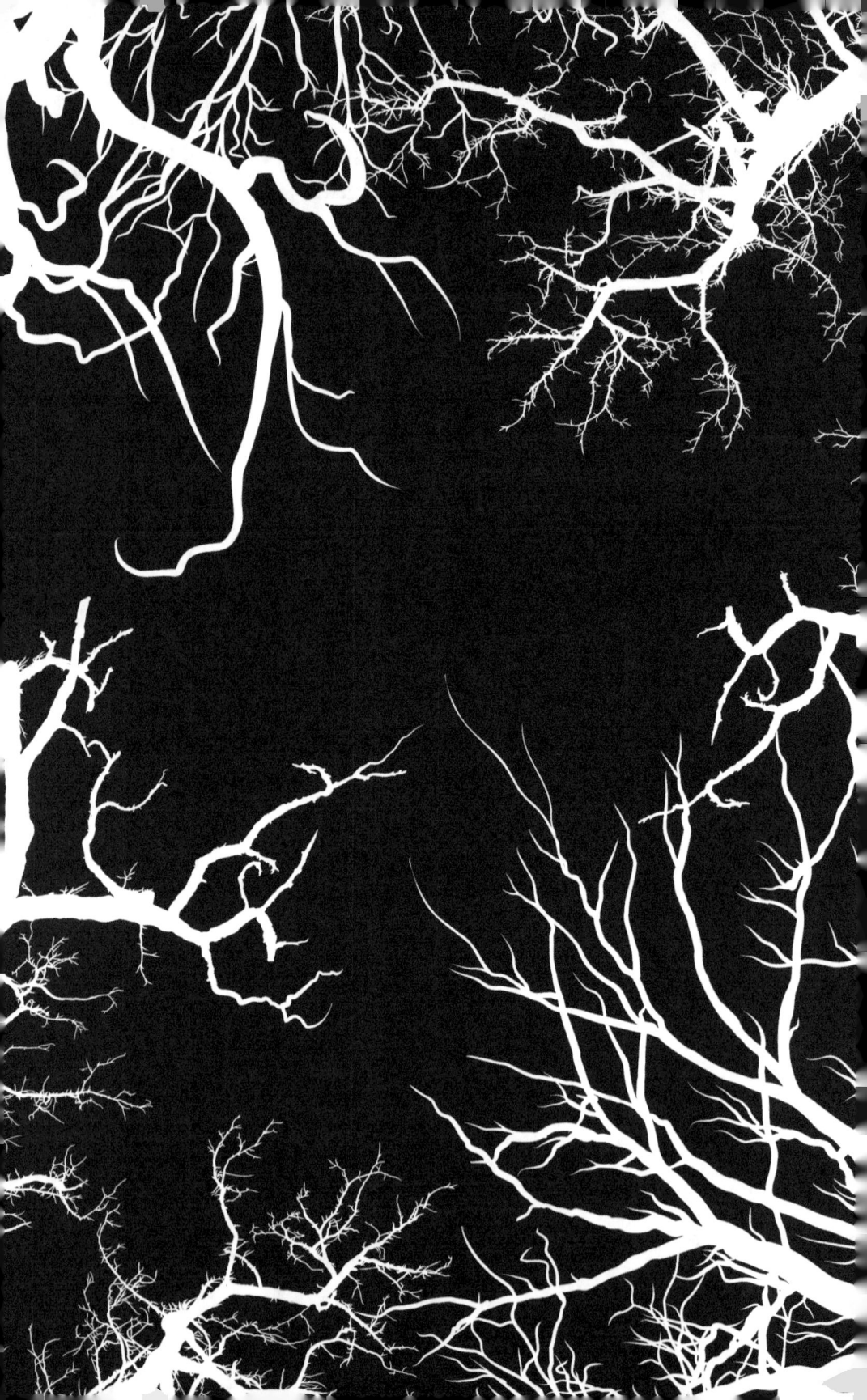

CHAPTER 6
OLIVIA

The room I'm in is a replica of the movie *Scream's* garage. Complete with an animatronic kicking their legs while being trapped in the garage door that looks as if it's going up and down. An unhinged laugh filters through the air as I search for the exit. Turning around, I realize I can't go out the way I came in because it's been closed off. How the hell did that happen? I didn't even hear it close.

My head spins trying to find how to leave this room. All I want is to get back home, put on my coziest pajamas, and pretend like this night never happened.

Distant screams keep penetrating the air, surrounding me as I finally spot the way out. It looks like I'll have to squeeze my body through the dangling mannequin's legs as they flail about.

"Where do you think you're going sweetie? Don't you want to play a game before you go?"

A figure dressed in the iconic *Ghostface* costume comes out of nowhere, I don't even know how he was able to get the sealed room, but his raised knife has me scrambling. My feet trip over the boxes and I come down hard, knees and palms kissing the ground. Fuck, it hurts.

The figure laughs darkly, getting close enough that he grabs me by my hair, knife to my throat. The cool steel makes me think for a brief second that it's real and fear floods my veins, making my entire body shake.

"P-please. Let me go," I'm not above begging. Tears sting at my eyes while the man pushes in closer, mask pressing against my ear while he crouches down over me.

"Mmm. I love the smell of your fear." He presses into my ass, and I can feel how hard he is.

"Get off me!" I yell, wishing that I hadn't let go of Callie's hand. Wishing I'd never even come here in the first place.

"No, little ghoul. I think you like it. I think you want to be fucked and touched." He runs his leather clad hands down my neck and spine as he sits right on my ass, pulling my hair and making my back arch until it hurts.

He presses into me, rocking on my body as I lay helpless beneath him. I can't even move my legs to kick him off.

My entire body shivers as he grinds himself into me, hitting that sensitive spot that has my skin feeling like it's on fire.

I need more.

God that's so fucked up. I haven't been touched in so long that I'm getting off from some twisted stranger in a Halloween mask.

The fear from earlier is replaced by a new ravenous emotion. A need for release.

He suddenly flips me over, knife gleaming in the strobe light.

"Smile pretty for me, little ghoul."

The mask gets uncomfortably close to my face as the knife is dragged down my face not hard enough to draw blood, but close enough that I can feel its sharp edge.

My heart beats erratically, stumbling over each pulse. It flutters full of fear and dread behind my ribs.

Suddenly, his weight is thrown off me and I'm able to scramble to a standing position.

Behind me a scuffle between the attacker and a blurry looking figure with gleaming gold horns ensues. I blink vigorously, wondering how hard he yanked my hair for me not to be seeing clearly. It dawns on me that I should run, but I can't seem to make myself move. Everything feels intangible, as if this isn't even real. But I know that it is. Deep in my bones, something tells me that what I'm seeing and experiencing is real.

The man who assaulted me lays motionless on the ground, with blood seeping from his head where the knife he once held now is embedded. The demon-like figure is nowhere to be seen.

Stunned, I creep closer and chance reaching down into the blood. My fingertips graze the crimson stained liquid, and my entire body immediately recoils.

It's warm.

It's real.

The other figure, the one who saved me, is nowhere to be found. Oh god. What if they think I did this?

Images of my kids being taken from me, as I end up in jail flicker through my mind's eye.

Fuck that.

I take off through the door, wiping the blood from my hands with a prayer to the universe on my lips that I can get the hell out of here unscathed.

"Callie!" I call out for my friend, as I dodge the opening of multiple morgue doors in the small hallway. They skim across my flesh as I pass. Cool metal that reeks of rotten meat. It takes everything in me not to retch on the floor right here.

"Help me!" A young woman's voice calls out, but I can't tell where it's coming from.

"Callie, is that you?" I keep running but a person jumps out, stopping me. I scream and push past, picking up the speed.

"You can run, but you can't hide, girlie."

My head is spinning, as I make a turn into another room of horrors, only this one is set up like a movie theater. A projector flashes images of some slasher movie while the people in the seats writhe and scream, their arms held down by restraints.

The reviews weren't fucking kidding. It *is* lifelike, and I'm starting to think maybe it's more real than I realize, though, I don't want to believe it. The blood from the man still stains my fingers, feeling sticky and smelling like a pungent old metal.

"Help!" the same woman's voice calls, only this time, it's closer.

She grabs my arms, fingernails digging into my flesh through the material on my sweatshirt.

"You have to help me. My boyfriend." She shakes me, tears streaming down her bruised face. "Th-they k-killed him."

"Get off of me, please. You're hurting me!" Her fingers dig in harder. "Let go!" I demand, not liking this one bit.

"They'll kill us too!" she cries, until someone jumps out

from the shadows and grabs her. She kicks and screams, fighting them, but they drag her through black dangling ribbons.

Someone grabs hold of my arm, and I scream again.

"Please, please help me."

They're wrapped up like a mummy and are covered in blood. Their arms are chained to the movie theater seat. Their hand is wet, and the gap for where their mouth should be is a wide black expanse. Wrenching my wrist away, I scramble backwards, bumping into a muscled body.

For a moment, I think it's the handsome stranger, until the scent of decay hits my nose. Looking up, I realize it's someone dressed as an all too realistic zombie. Their eyes are pitch black and their skin is peeling away from their face, revealing parts of their skull and bits of muscle. Sections of their molted skin have been sewn back on in a crude fashion by someone clearly unfamiliar with how to work a thread and needle. What hair they have left is gray and attached in clumps.

As soon as they open their mouth, a lime green mist expels from it, hitting my face and rendering me speechless.

I can't scream.

I can't even fucking blink.

Staring wide eyed at the beast before me, a cruel smirk takes over its patched together face. A pustule covered tongue licks up my neck and I feel every bump as the slime coats my skin. Revulsion and vomit climb up my throat, but I'm too frozen to do anything about it.

"You taste like strawberries and..." He licks the other side of my neck trailing my pounding jugular. "Mmm. Mint. I'm going to have so much fun, sucking on your brains. I bet they taste just as sweet."

A scream comes from the screen, flickering images of a woman getting stabbed over and over again in the stomach. My knees begin to quake, and I realize, maybe I'm not as frozen as I thought. Sure enough, my leg is able to move, and I yank it up, hitting him right in the balls. A loud cracking noise erupts from the contact as he lets me go, clutching at his injured parts.

Shoving him, I make a break for the slit between the theater curtains and take off down another dark hallway and into the claws of a shrouded priest.

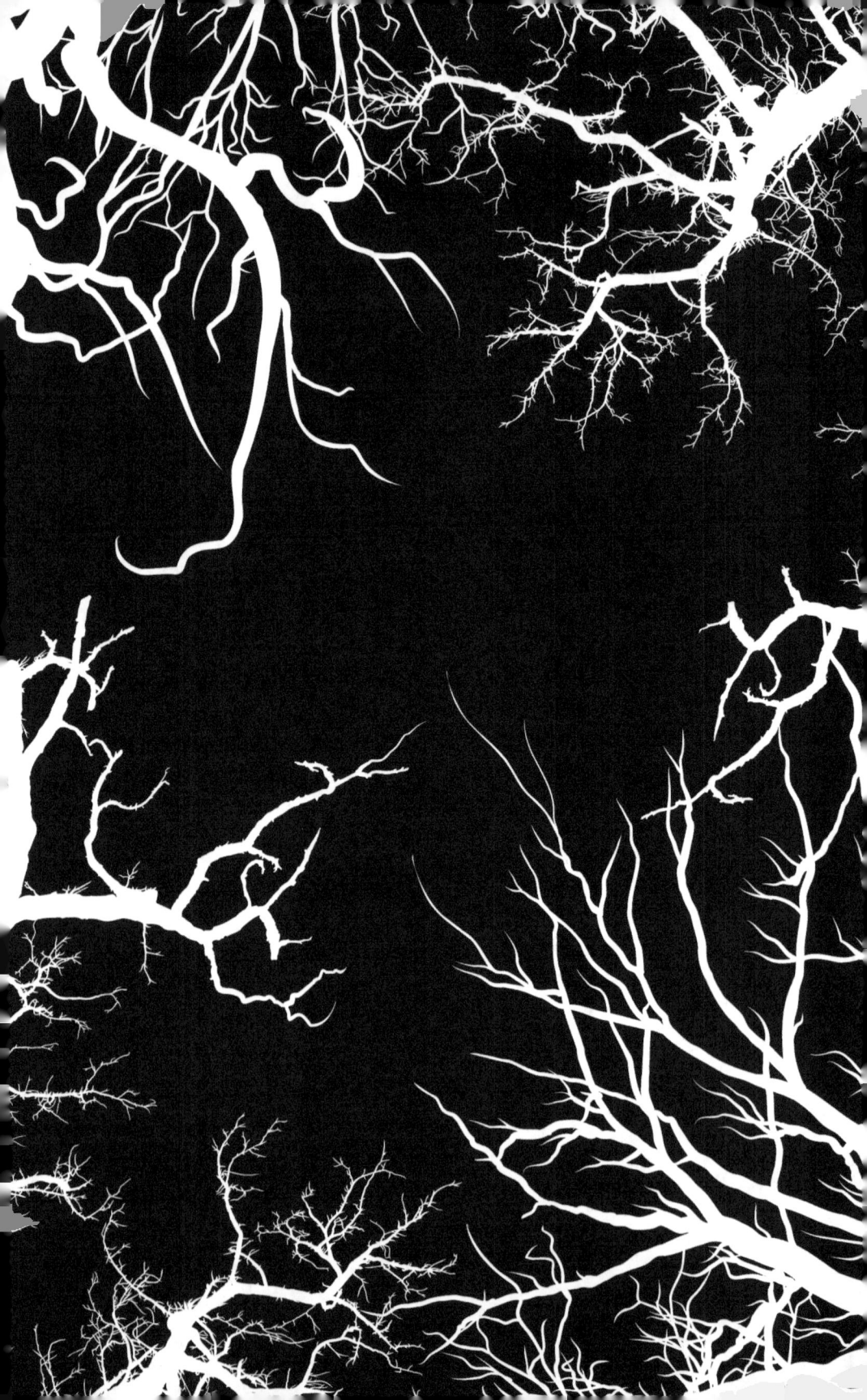

CHAPTER 7
TALON

T he church is one of my favorite additions to the wicked work of art I call my home. And truthfully, the only place I feel I can spread my wings. It's a twisted, perverse version meant to inflict fear and torment on all who enter.

Blessed be the soul who escapes such a place as ours.

My leathery black wings carry me through the many rooms, flying past the shrieks and screams of our patrons here to revel in the darkness. They get off on being frightened by my monsters. Freeing themselves to the rush that their adrenaline brings as it pumps wildly through their deliciously corrupt veins. Their blood tastes that much sweeter with every scream their breakable little necks produce.

I bank hard to the left, transforming into my full vampire form before a cluster of yelping young girls who scurry away in fright. One thing that I love about the place I've created, is knowing that no one trusts what they see here. I can get away with murder in broad daylight and no one blinks an eye, considering it all part of an act. And with the witch's spells pumping through the vents, the mortal's distorted perceptions of reality are constantly working against their senses. Allowing for us to go undetected.

We make them see and believe what we want them to.

It helps that the human brain is so easily pliable. Like putty in my hands. Always working to believe the easiest explanation, because the alternative is too much to stomach. That monsters are in fact, real and roaming amongst them. And we're worse than they could ever imagine.

The girl we plan to share is crying thick streaks of mascara down her gorgeous face with a blood red tint to her skin cast from the ghoulish lighting above. One of the demonic priests named, Asmodious, forces her to her knees by her throat. His black horns are on full display while a white collar and black robs hang haphazardly across his hunched form.

"Confess your sins or be sent to Hell," Asmodious threatens, digging his gnarled claws into her supple skin. I stand back with my arms folded over my chest watching the scene unfold. It's rare that I participate in the revelry, choosing instead to observe from above. But tonight, I feel the pull.

"For fucks sake, let me go!" She begs, clawing at his mottled skin.

A fighter, then. The knowledge of this revelation pleases me.

As soon as she arrived on the grounds, I felt her. The shift in the air, the allure of her sweet little soul. A rare gem amongst the sludge.

"You'll confess or pay the price."

Her skin begins to darken several shades of red as the demon priest tightens his hold on her delicate neck.

"That's enough, demon," my voice booms, causing the performer to startle. He drops the girl, and she falls in a spectacular heap on the hard ground. She looks up at me, tears still clinging to her long lashes and bottom lip quivering.

A beautiful fucking mess.

"Th-thank you," she says, standing up with a shiver. The fear she exhibits is delicious. I can hear the way her heart pumps from here, shooting blood to her organs and extremities. My fangs lengthen at the thought of getting a taste.

"You shouldn't thank me, little ghoul. In fact, you should run so I can have the pleasure of catching you."

Her eyes widen and that plump mouth of hers drops open. Inhaling her sweet scent, I use my mind to peer into hers, shuffling through her thoughts easily to find the one thing I need.

"Run, Olivia!" I command, altering my voice to inflict my power upon her and feeling her name coat my lips.

Unsurprisingly, she obeys, not even stopping to wonder how I know her name.

She bends so beautifully to my will.

It's been far too long since I've had a proper chase. A chance to indulge in my monstrous instincts. I've been too busy running this place to really give into my nature. But tonight, on Halloween, her bright soul calls to me. Begging to be tormented and taken.

I'm going to stuff her cunt so full she'll be begging for mercy.

But I'm not feeling particularly merciful tonight.

Not in the least.

A rumble of excitement rattles about my chest as I wait, giving her a five second head start before following her into my playground. As soon as the time is up, I take off, darting through the maze of rooms and following the thunderous beat of her heart. Her screams penetrate the air sounding like a sweet symphony of terror.

My nostrils flare with excitement as I track her down, flitting past the scent of decay, I find her easily, sliding up behind her faster than she has time to blink. There isn't time for her to block my advance as I cage her against the hallway wall. We're all alone here. Plunged into darkness with only a sliver of light to illuminate. Not that I need the light to make out her features. I thrive in the dark.

"Olivia," I test the sound of her name again against her ear, chest flush against her supple curves. Her nipples poke hard through her sweatshirt telling me she's enjoying this— being scared and chased. She's turned on. I can smell her desire rolling off her in waves.

It's intoxicating.

I want to drink it down or bathe in it.

"H-how do you know my name?" She asks, skin trembling beneath my fingers.

"I know all kinds of things." I drag my fingers through her hair, tilting her head so that she has to look directly at me. "I can see those deep dark thoughts you think you've buried. The ones where you imagine hitting your dead-beat ex with your car. How you like to rewind it over and over again in your mind, watching his brains splatter across the windshield." A shiver runs down my spine as I uncover her twisted secrets. "I can see your wildest fantasies, how you long to be taken, and used, and fucked within an inch of your life. Would you like to see how that feels, Olivia? To have all your tight little holes filled?" My hand roams the length of her neck, feeling her pulse thump wildly beneath the pads of my fingertips. Immediately, my fangs lengthen wanting to sink into her skin and suck from the delicious crimson river that runs through her veins.

Her moss green eyes go wide, and she licks her plump lips, fixated on my mouth. I know she's watching my canines. Her thoughts run wild wondering what they would feel like against her skin.

My little ghoul is braver than she gives herself credit for.

"Found you," Phantom exclaims, interrupting us.

"Took you long enough," I reply.

With how busy it is, I'm surprised I had her to myself this long.

Olivia takes in the two of us connecting the dots, her thoughts whirring inside her head a million miles a minute. Almost too fast for me to catch. But I'm able to make out a whisper of a thought that has my cock hardening in my pants.

She wants us.

She might be scared of her mind, but there's no denying her curiosity and desire.

A rumble of feet pounding against the floor approaches, vibrating the ground beneath our feet.

Time's up.

"Olivia, darling, open that pretty little throat up for me and scream."

She doesn't have a chance to see the hidden panel opening

up behind her to swallow her whole. As the door closes her scream echoes off the walls as she falls down into my lair. Trapped like a rat in a cage.

"Where did you send her?" Phantom asks, looking miffed.

"Somewhere she can't escape."

CHAPTER 8
OLIVIA

My entire body is free falling in pure darkness as a scream rips free from my throat. I don't know which way is up as I careen down, down, down, until I crumple against something plush that envelops me. Catching my fall ever so gently that it surprises me.

I was sure I was about to end up a crumpled mess of blood and bones, but instead there's nothing but a soft pillowy expanse to shield me from that twisted fate.

My mind is a jumbled mess of fear and desire. A combination I never thought I could feel. There's an eeriness that hangs about this place and the people here that make me wonder if there's something more going on. Something I'm not piecing together.

As if on cue, a door opens, and a small sliver of light illuminates the space I'm in. A heavy shuffling pierces the quiet and I fold in on myself, waiting for whatever it could be to emerge from the shadows.

"Master has gifted us a present. A pretty little present indeed," a disembodied voice says.

Goosebumps erupt all over my skin at the way the voice stalks closer. Whatever it is, I can't see it, but it feels like it's right on top of me. Hot breath tickles my face, smelling of onions. My raw vocal cords manage to shriek as I swat uselessly at the air to no avail.

Whatever it is grips onto my wrists and wraps a restraint around both, pinning me down before moving to my ankles. I'm stuck here. Spread wide and unable to move.

"Back away from her, Killspree, she's mine." The man that shoved me down here enters the space in a blur of speed. His presence exudes a level of attraction I've never felt before. He's alluring and dangerous, making me feel like he could easily murder me while fucking my brains out and not feel an ounce of remorse. I don't know why that thought turns me on.

I should be frightened by him.

But the way he held me turned me to putty in his large hands, and I wanted to feel them on me again. Even though he pushed me, I'm decidedly unharmed, so there is that.

He's well dressed. Too well dressed for a place like this. Though, admittedly he's handsome as all hell with that stark gray streak of hair that sits right over his ear. It makes me want to run my fingers through it.

My muddled mind quickly forgets all the fear pumping through my veins and focuses in on this specimen of a man. He eats up my vision making the expansive room melt away. All I can see is him.

Then, the man that was helping me earlier, steps in behind him and a tendril of anticipation runs through my core. They're looking at me like I am their prey that they've caught and intend to devour.

Licking my lips, I watch as the taller man closes the door, trapping me in here with them. That's when I look around nervously and note the vaulted ceilings and gothic architecture that makes up the room. It's haunting and otherworldly. Almost like it's been transported from another time. The space is eerily quiet. A stark difference from the rooms above. That was the stuff of nightmares, but down here I feel like I can finally relax.

Belatedly, I realize that what I've fallen onto is a bed. Complete with black silk sheets and a multitude of pillows. It's soft, and welcoming, and the way it caresses my skin is downright sinful. Though, I'm still restrained.

"What do you want to do to me? Are you going to free me?" I ask, sprawled out like a meal before these two imposing specimens.

"We want to stuff your holes so full, little ghoul, you'll be screaming for us to stop. And I think you're just fine the way you are. Spread so nicely for us."

My heart stutters in my chest at that confession.

"I don't even know your names."

"Does it matter?"

That question roams the length of my brain as they make it to the edge of the bed.

Suddenly, the man from earlier disappears completely in the blink of an eye and I let out a scream.

"Where the fuck did he go?" I ask pulling at the restraints, only to be met with a smirk from the one that pushed me down here.

"I'm right here," his voice answers in my right ear. I jump and look to where the noise came from, but there's nothing.

Oh god, this was a terrible idea to come here. I must be having some sort of mental break down, or this place is equipped with the world's most convincing special effects to make people see what they want.

True and real terror grips hold of my chest and my heart rate triples from the fright. A ghost of a touch caresses my check, and my hair is tucked gently behind my ear as short stuttering breaths break free of my shaking chest.

"Your fear is delectable, my little ghoul. I can't wait to swallow those screams of yours."

Muscles shaking, I see the man appear slowly, as if pieces of him are knitting together before my very eyes.

"What are you?" I ask, bewildered by what my own eyes are seeing.

He turns fully corporeal and grabs my chin before pulling me closer to him, nearly a breath a part before he whispers, "A monster." His lips close over mine and I find myself pushed back with force and kissing him back.

I should be shoving him off me- trying to break free and getting the hell out of here with a scream on my lips and fear in my heart, but I can't. All I can do is succumb to the feeling of his mouth on mine. I want more, so much more.

I'm too enthralled with the feeling of him that I don't notice the other man dipping into the bed next to me until his hands are roaming the length of my body. Moaning, I break the kiss and look over at him. His fangs are on display as his long fingers play with the hem of my hoodie. The coolness of his skin slides along the warmth of mine sending a shiver down my spine.

"We're going to take such good care of you," he promises, and for some reason, I believe him.

I've never been one to take someone at their word without knowing them before, but there's a sincerity in his voice, and an intensity in his gaze that makes me want to grant him my trust. His dark hair tumbles over his brow as his lift my hand to his mouth and I watch, captivated, wondering what he's going to do next.

He takes my pointer finger into his mouth and sucks it into his mouth, surprising me at how good and sensual that small little act feels. His tongue runs the length of my finger, and a riot of butterflies gathers deep in my core.

I am but a fly caught in the web of these monsters, and I'm afraid I like it.

"Tell us what you want, Olivia," the man on my other side asks, running his ghostly hand through my hair.

Maybe this isn't real after all. Perhaps I've hit my head and am dreaming this all up. Being the object of attention for these two handsome creatures, I hesitate to call them men because there's something, other, about them. Something dark, and dangerous, and thrilling.

"I want..."

"Yes?" I feel the brush of fangs scraping against my neck. Sharp. Lethal. Fucking hot as hell.

"I want to be fucked." There. I said it, and it's the truth. I'm tired of pretending like I don't have needs. Tired of being strong for everyone else. I want to be selfish, and if this isn't real, then who the hell cares if I'm contemplating letting two hot as hell strangers fuck me senseless?

"That we can do," the one to my right answers, shrugging off his leather jacket and pulling off his white t-shirt in one swift move. I'm treated to the most stunning display of washboard abs with a perfect v that cuts into his narrow hips. My mouth drops open and it's clear he likes my reaction by the smirk that takes over his handsome face.

Oh God, this is really happening, isn't it?

My pussy aches with need, wanting them inside me right now. It doesn't matter which one. Or both, hell, having given birth twice maybe it could work.

As I watch him discard his pants, the one with fangs starts to remove my shoes, then goes for my leggings. Peeling them off me oh so slowly. Torturously so. When he gets to the point he can no longer pull, a long claw emerges like a knife at the edge of his hand. He savors the moment, dragging it down the length of my plush thighs. It lights me up inside, burning a tendril of desire into a raging inferno of lust before he rips into the material, shredding it to bits. Next, his finger slices through my panties, the cool brush of his skin feels like icicles as he rubs against my clit.

"We're going to have so much fun with you, Olivia. I can scent just how wet you are for us already." He inhales my discarded panties, dropping my legs. An inhumane rumble erupts from his chest. Why the fuck do I find that sound so hot? It immediately has me clenching my thighs together with the little give I have from the restraints, seeking some friction for how turned on I am right now.

"Oh no, none of that." He grips my legs apart viciously. "If you're going to find release, it's going to be at the hands of one of us."

A small moan escapes my throat as his hands wander up the length of my stomach, slicing my favorite hoodie up the middle. I didn't wear a bra thinking the hoodie would be plenty coverage. That's the good thing about fall and winter clothes, the boobs can hang free, and no one gives a shit because they can't tell. But now, that decision has come to stare me in the face as both men hone in on my naked body, breasts fully on display. Heavy with want, and nipples pulled into two tight peaks, aching to be played with.

"You're a fucking angel," the one who's discarded his clothes states, and by the way he stares at me, makes me believe he truly means it. I light up under his praise, feeling adored and appreciated. The feeling is foreign, but a welcome change from never feeling good enough. Skinny enough. Pretty enough.

Shortly after I had the girls, Trent left for someone younger, claiming I had let myself go. But the way these two look at me, make me feel like Trent was wrong. I am desirable.

"That's right, my sweet little ghoul. You are desirable." Oh right, this one can read my fucking thoughts. My cheeks heat and I nibble nervously on my bottom lip. "And I'm going to make sure you don't forget it." He slips out of the bed, and discards his clothing so quickly, it seems I'm watching it at two times the speed. Fuck, my mind and senses are so frazzled to the point of snapping. I don't know if what I'm seeing is truly what's happening or if it's just the effect this place has.

"Please, tell me your name," I beg of them. The vents kick in whirring a fine mist into the air and a heady sensation takes over me. My skin crawls with the need to be touched.

"Names have power my sweet. Are you sure you can handle it?" I'm not sure who's speaking in the haze. Tendrils of fog warp the room in a vertigo like state.

I lick my lips. "Yes, please."

"She's so damn polite. Think we can break her of it, Talon?"

"Absolutely. I plan to make that sweet mouth praise my cock like she was born to worship it."

They snicker but the name turns over in my mind. "Talon," I say, only to have the man the name belongs to whip his head in my direction and end up centimeters away from my face. Knees planted on both sides of my hips.

"Say it again, little ghoul."

"Talon," I oblige and watch his deep amber eyes alight with what looks like a flame surrounding his pupil. It's mesmerizing and a little frightening. I might be in over my head, never having done something like this before, but damn do I want to try.

"You like playing with fire?" he asks, shoving the tip of his large cock against my opening. "Then I'll burn you from the inside out."

I want to reach out and grab him, but the restraints make that impossible. He teases himself against my slick entrance. Taking his time to taunt me, rubbing against my swollen clit. Toying with me like a cat playing with a mouse before devouring it whole.

"Please," I beg. "Talon, fuck me."

The light in his eyes flares right before he slams into me

forcibly. Desperately. My eyes roll back into my head as his cock hits so deep I think it brushes against my cervix.

"Eyes on me as I take what belongs to me," Talon demands.

Phantom watches from the side, stroking his considerable length.

"And what's that?" I ask.

"Your soul," he responds, pistoning his hips against mine.

CHAPTER 9

TALON

It's been years since I've felt this alive. This enticed by another. And to be sharing this experience with two others is a delectable surprise. It's not at all how I'd planned to spend my night, but a welcome change all the same.

She feels like a warm summer day wrapped around my dick, a blessing I haven't had the pleasure of experiencing since I was human. Her tight pussy takes me so well. She's tight, and wet, and moves in time with every thrust I dish out to her. Her moans fill my head with dark and depraved ideas.

I want to consume her every moan her thin throat utters, drinking them down like I'm dying of thirst, and she is the only thing that can quench my desire.

Her beautiful eyes bore into me, watching as I take her, but her gaze isn't the only one I'm interested in. Phantom stares as if he can't look away at the display playing out before him. I can tell he wishes it were him fucking Olivia right now, but he'll have to wait his turn. She's mine to claim. Mine to fuck. Mine to ruin.

And then when Phantom has had his fill, I'll claim him too. Reminding him of who owns his soul.

The restraints have her spread for me so perfectly, I can see every curve of her luscious body. Every divot, and swell splayed out for my pleasure. She's at my mercy, and I'm fresh out of being capable of restraint.

She's walked into a den of monsters and become a fly caught in our web of dark desires. I'm easing her into it, afraid if I push her too early, she'll break. I want her whole and aware as I taint her unblemished soul.

The need to drink from her is overpowering as her tight cunt squeezes me, milking my cock for all I have to give. "Fuck. You feel so good wrapped around me, little ghoul." My fangs scrape her neck as I take in her scent. She smells like sin and sex. A delectable combination that has my cock growing even harder.

"Oh fuck!" she cries out, flailing against the restraints. Her thoughts scream with the desire to touch me, to push me into her harder. I smirk knowing how much she's enjoying this and decide to push her over the edge by using my vampire speed. I start out slow and ramp up my movements until I'm completely vibrating against her clit, filling her to the brink.

Her screams fill my ears, and I can't take it anymore, my fangs slice into her supple neck, drinking her sweet blood and bringing my orgasm and hers to a cataclysmic crescendo. The pleasure heightens between us as my teeth are lodged in her, mixing our orgasms together.

My breathing comes back to normal, and I remove my fangs

from her skin, running my fingers over the openings. They close at my touch as if they'd never been there, except for the silvery thin scars that remain.

Gathering the rope in my hands I let her restraints fall. She looks completely sated, but we're not done with her yet.

"Phantom, show me just how much you've been craving our little ghoul."

He takes his thick cock in hand, running it down his length and over the tip gathering the bead of pre-cum on his palm before working it down his dick. The sight is so unbelievably seductive.

I've observed Phantom from afar, always admiring his fine physique objectively. But now that he's here before me, I feel a surge of lust I wish to extort from him. Watching him run his hands over our girl, is a sight that I want to play back in my memories forever. She's so responsive, arching her body at his feather-light touch. He dips his fingers into her dripping hot cunt and gathers the evidence of her and my cum, coating himself in us before he shoves those drenched digits into his mouth.

Fuck ,that's hot.

I feel myself growing hard again watching them together. Olivia beckons to me, and I can't help myself. I'm drawn to them both, dropping into the bed next to them, touching their sweaty, sensuous bodies.

My hands find their way to Phantom's throbbing dick.

"Are you only good at sucking blood, Talon? Or can you manage a little meat in your mouth,"he taunts.

A growl rips free from my throat. "Is that a challenge?"

He thrusts into my hand, with a smirk dancing across his lips. "You tell me, boss."

"I think you're going to regret those words." I kneel between his strong thighs and place my mouth over him letting my tongue lick the underside of his sizable length. I trace his prominent vein up from base to tip, circling his mushroom shaped edge before allowing him deep into my throat.

"Oh fuck," he groans, threading his hand into my dark hair.

His salty taste explodes over my tastebuds as my fangs drag lightly against him. I could bite him. Mix the taste of cum and blood, but I want to see how well he takes our girl. I let him off with a loud pop and look deeply into those icy blue eyes of his, feeling the depths of my coercion settling over him before I give my command. "Now, I want to see you fuck our little ghoul until she comes at least three times."

Olivia's mouth drops, having been watching us intently this whole time. She was enjoying the show so much that she couldn't help but touch herself, a fact I confirm by seeing her snatch her hand away from her clit like she's just touched a hot burner.

"Don't be ashamed. Seeing you enjoy yourself is a goddamn turn on," Phantom reassures her and by the blush spreading up her neck, I can tell she's not used to being praised. "Now turn over, Olivia, let me see that beautiful ass of yours that's been taunting me all night."

She nods, settling herself in front of me as I rest against the headrest, cock at full attention. She clocks my hard cock and licks her lips. Her ass sticks up in the air for Phantom and he enters her from behind, making her shriek.

I take advantage of that open mouth and shove her down onto my length, shutting her scream up with my hard cock.

"You wanted to be taken by a pair of monsters, little ghoul, your wish is fucking granted." I shove her all the way down, watching her skin turn the most delicious shade of purple as she struggles against me. Phantom can't stop this compulsion, jackhammering into her hard and fast, balls slapping against her sweaty skin. Each thrust sends her mouth down further, taking my length deep as tears leak from her eyes.

Her thoughts begin to panic as her body begs for air. I let her take a breath before working her back down to where she belongs. Her fear and desire wage a war, but ultimately her desire wins out, letting herself give into our game. Taking me like she was made to. Her teeth scrape the underside of my cock, but the pain only fuels my harshness with her. I grip into her hair, pulling tight and rocking up into her mouth. "Fucking take it, Olivia. Swallow me down."

Her body shakes as she struggles against us both. Phantom from the back and me in the front. A gorgeous freaking sight.

Watching her heavy tits sway as she falters around me, has my second orgasm of the night building. I want to mark up those tits with bite marks, ones that leave a shimmery silver scar all along her flesh, marking her as mine.

Phantom's endless thrusts finally send her over the edge, making her moan around me. The vibrations do me in and I send a shot of hot cum down her tight throat. She swallows me down easily, drinking ever last drop before coming back up for air. Her orgasm rolls into another and another, finally collapsing on top of me, with Phantom not far behind.

We lay there, dazed for a moment- lost in a post-coital

bliss. Limbs entangled in each other before, I roll her to the side.

"Spread those legs for me, Olivia. I want to taste us." She welcomes my instruction too tired to refuse. She's a vision covered in sweat making her skin shimmer in the firelight.

I lean down on my forearms and lick her sensitive clit, tasting a mixture of me, Phantom, and her. I can't help but let my fangs loose, biting the plump area around her slit and tasting her blood.

"AHhh, mmff," Olivia mutters, giving into the sensation as I suck and lick, giving her just the right amount of pressure before I have her coming on my tongue again. Her legs are quivering against my head, which will make what I have planned next all the more fun.

"Olivia, I want you to put that shirt on over there." I command, fixing her with every inch of my compulsion. "And then I want you to run. Run until we catch you. *Now.*"

Her eyes go wide as she watches me transform before her into a bat. She scrambles out of the bed, fear gripping her throat as she obeys, throwing the oversized shirt on and sprinting for the door.

I give her the head-start she needs before following her into the dark. Besides, she can't escape unless I want her to, and right now, she's my prisoner. My prey. My little ghoul.

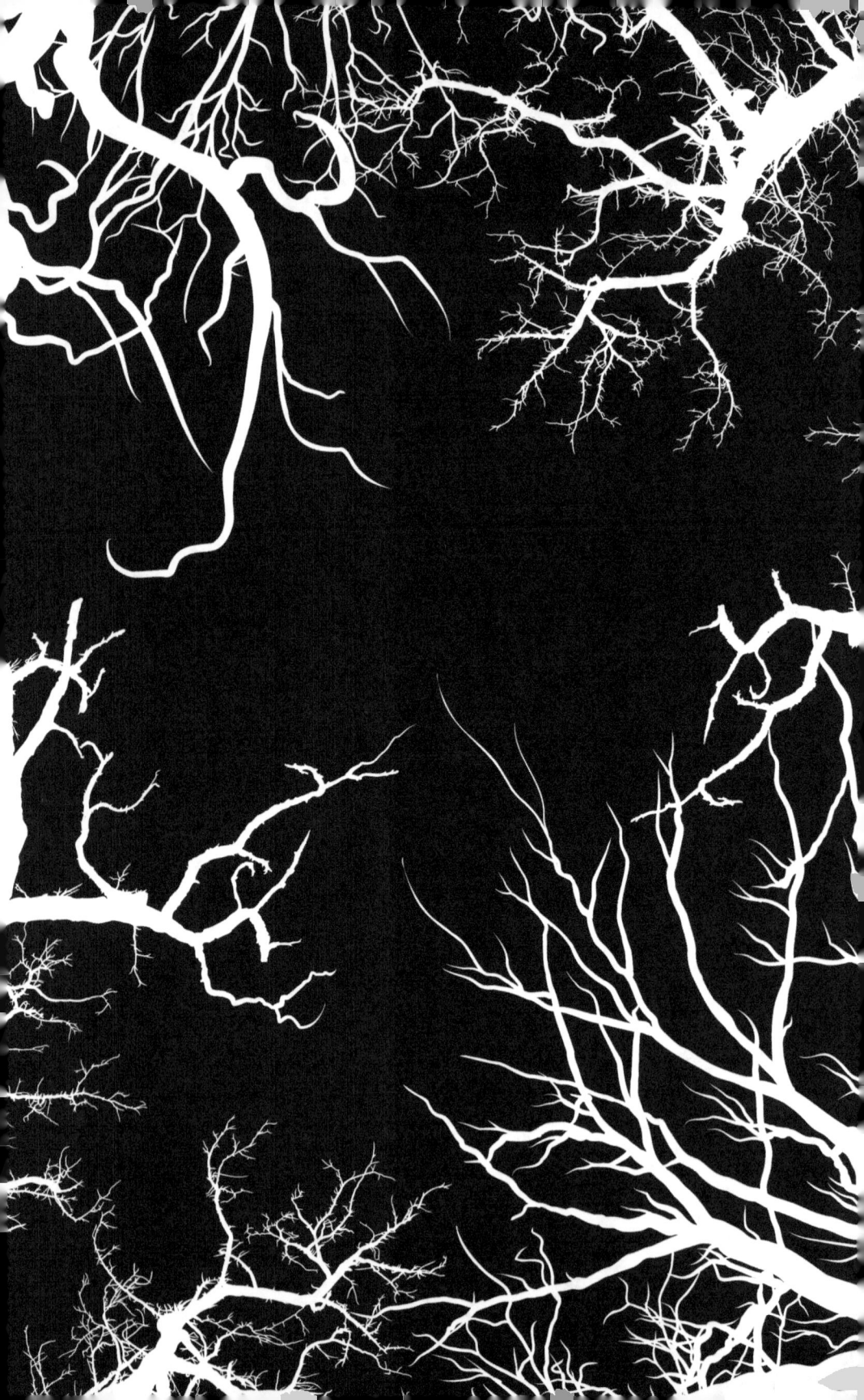

CHAPTER 10
OLIVIA

The command to run reverberates through my whole body. Muscles obeying, pumping the blood through my veins of their own volition. The rooms blur together as I dash past, trying, once again, to find the exit. This place is a never-ending labyrinth. Groups of people dressed in costumes move out of my way as my legs carry me in a daze. My body echoes with the pleasure Talon and Phantom elicited from me. Pleasure like I've never experienced before.

And those bites...

My fingers graze the skin on my neck and feel two slim indents. The skin is closed, but the whisper of what transpired lingers. I don't know which way to run, and no one else seems to know the right way either. Groups of people head in different directions through dark and terrifying rooms filled with screams. Some of the rooms, though, have devolved into a free for all. Fucking up against the sticky walls amongst fallen figures and frightening animatronics. A fine mist of fog rolls steadily along the floor so thick I can't see my feet. It smells of sex, sweat, and blood.

Distracted, I turn down another dark corner, but as I do, my body collides into a tall figure, startling the breath right out of me. They turn around and I take in the familiar white mask from *Scream*, only now a knife is lodged into their skull and a shiver of fear runs down my spine. Oh fuck. How are they still alive?

"Y-you're dead," I say, stupidly. Clearly, they're walking around, all alive and breathing.

"No," they chuckle, pushing me back into the wall, using their height to tower over me. "But you? You won't be so lucky." They pull the knife from their head, blood dripping down the length of the sharp tip landing in fat, wet splotches across my cheeks.

The knife barrels down towards me and a scream rips from my throat. I close my eyes and brace for impact, but nothing happens. Instead, I see the knife plunged into the wall behind my head.

"Wh-what?" I ask, dumbfounded.

"You didn't think I'd end you so easily, did you? Not when we were so rudely interrupted before." His hands run down my body. I'm still sensitive from earlier, but I can't help but lean into him. This masked figure, who I should be running from, knows just how to touch me. Making me want him. That seems to be the theme for the night. My inner slut is at the helm, and I have to just hold on for the ride, hoping that bitch isn't going to steer me wrong. His hands grip firmly around my breast, kneading them in his hands as he presses his hips against mine. I can feel every inch of him through the thin shirt I'm wearing.

It lands just beneath my ass, exposing my long legs. I feel myself wrapping my leg around his waist as he thrust up against me.

"I knew you were a little horny slut. Wanting to play with the monsters. Mmm you smell like sex," he says mask mere inches from my face.

My fingers come up to the edge of the mask and an unspoken agreement passes between us as I yank it off, revealing one of the hottest guys I've ever seen in my life. Though, I can't help but notice the two gleaming black horns jutting out from the top of his head.

"Matchbox, what the fuck are you doing with my girl?" Phantom's voice calls from down the hall. A rattling of screams wafts through the air and a distant "Help me" that sounds vaguely like Callie echoes around me. This place is sensory overload, playing with my mind, making me question my own experiences. I hardly know what's real or not anymore.

As far as I know, those monsters I just fucked could have been just a figment of my imagination, though the ache in between my legs tells me otherwise. But then, that would mean if it really did happen, then monsters are real, and I'm walking amongst them. Not just walking, enjoying... fucking. God, I want more already, and it hasn't even been ten minutes.

"Don't get your panties in a twist. She was liking it. Weren't you, sweetheart?"

It's dark in here, but the flashing strobe light illuminates enough I think they can see the blush staining my cheeks. I was liking it. Hell, if Phantom hadn't walked in, I might have let his friend fuck me right up against this wall. Fuck, who even am I right now? It must be this place, making me act like this, so out of character, and sluggish. Thoughts jumbled into a mess of lust and fear.

"Talon's claimed her as ours, Matchbox, so she's off limits," Phantom says, jabbing his friend in the chest with his finger.

"Ugh, no. Sorry, but no one owns me," I say shakily. "I've been down that road before and ended up with a divorce and a calloused heart. I belong to me and me alone." Hands on my hips, I take in their shocked appearance, and decide I rather like it. They may be real monsters, but apparently, I've found my fucking backbone.

"Didn't I tell you to run?" Talon's voice whispers in my ear, sending a wave of goosebumps down my body. His commanding presence eats up the remaining space in this otherwise cramped hallway.

"I did," I say, turning around to catch a hint of a smile on his imposing figure. "I can't help it if someone else caught me first. Guess, you're getting slow, old man." A flash of fire erupts in his eyes and a low guttural growl escapes his chest.

Maybe I'm playing with fire, but if that means feeling adored, then I'll stoke those embers happily. I might not recognize myself after tonight, but I think I'm liking whoever I'm becoming.

"Let's try this again, little ghoul. I want you to fucking run so I can tackle you to the ground and shove my dick in your panting, scared little cunt, until you scream your throat raw."

I look up at him and go up on my tip toes to bring his face level with mine.

"Deal." I kiss him, surprising him, before I take off running at full speed and into the depths of the haunted house.

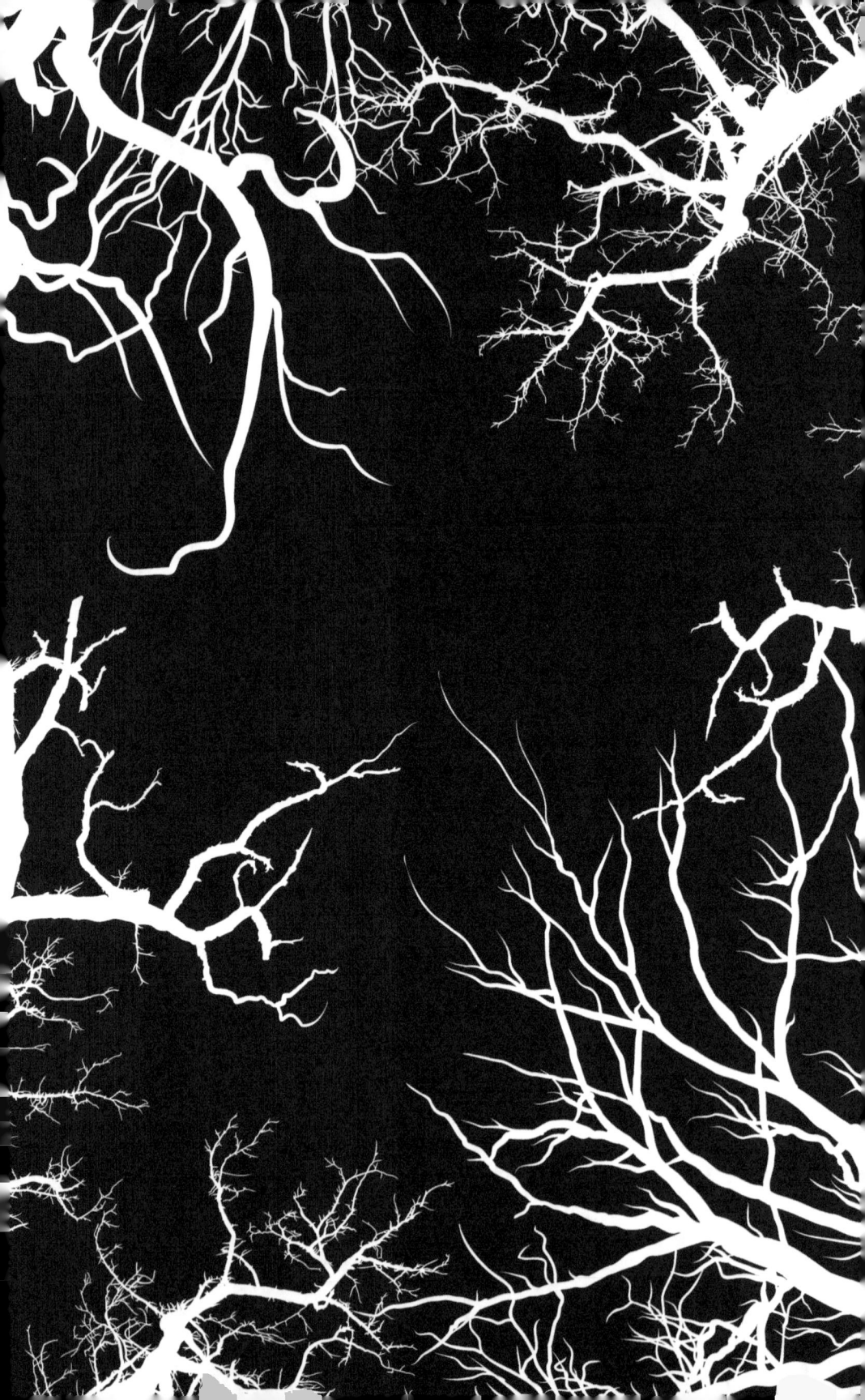

CHAPTER 11

PHANTOM

Her scent mixed with mine and Talon's, permeates the air and it isn't hard to pick up on where she's going. A few more turns and she'll be spit out into the corn maze. My personal favorite that this place has to offer. Although, in the summer when we can run along the grounds at all hours of the day and night is a close second.

I'm practically buzzing with the thrill of the chase. Hunting her down is in my blood. It's in all of our nature here. At least those of us that are cursed to serve out our sentencing here. Allowed to roam, but not escape. Having Olivia, though, is making me regret that particular set of terms and conditions.

Note to self— always read the goddamn fine print.

Matchbox trails behind, inserting himself like a fucking parasite. But how can I blame him? Our girl is like a siren. Calling to us with her sweet as fuck song, drawing us in like moths to a flame.

She's irresistible.

The witches spell holds strong on her, like it does all mortals that dare to visit the haunted house. It whirs through the vents wafting into the human's weak lungs and absorbing right into their bloodstream, making them our pliable little puppets. Aware enough, but easy to manipulate.

The ghost in me relishes this chase. Wanting more of her and the way she felt wrapped around my cock. It's been longer than I care to admit since someone has touched me like that, and not only did she unlock this primal need, but Talon has also wormed his way into my thoughts. Surprising me with his wickedly talented mouth.

Fuck, that vampire can suck dick.

Having my hot as fuck, and centuries old boss get on his knees for me is fucking with my head, making me want a repeat.

"Which way did she go?" Matchbox asks. He's not as adept at tracking as I am, being newer to his demon form. The older we get, the more we hone our monstrous skills. That's why Talon is the best of us, being the oldest motherfucker here.

"Who invited you?" Talon asks, transforming in front of our eyes. His demeanor is deadly and determined. A predator in the midst of stalking his precious prey.

Matchbox silently points at me, and I roll my eyes. Talon seems mildly irritated by the way his shoulders tense, but after a beat, he relents, not wanting to waste precious time with Olivia.

"Fine. But don't let me regret it." He says, turning back into a bat and rounding the corner.

The exit is right up ahead, and Olivia is right at the cusp, hands poised over the bar that will have her stumbling out of here and into the night air.

Gotcha.

She turns just in time to see the three of us converging on her. We're almost within reach.

A small smile tugs at that plush mouth of hers, before she slips out of the door. It shuts with a shudder, as if the house is offended by the intrusion. My hands reach the bar, pressing down with all my might, but it won't budge.

"The hell?"

"Move," Talon demands, shoving me out of the way, but the door refuses to give. "Open this door at once, house," he yells, but a rumble of power rolls under our feet, opening a chasm in the floor and sucking all three of us down into the bowels of the decaying basement.

Talon, at least, is able to catch his fall by using his wings, but I and Matchbox weren't as quick. I'd been in my corporeal form, a decision I'm regretting as I take in my backwards set leg. Agony rips down my nerves as I adjust the limb to where it's supposed to be, then quickly change into my ghost form. Fuck that. In my ghost form I can't feel a goddamn thing, and sometimes that comes in handy.

"What the hell just happened?" Matchbox asks, rubbing his horns.

"We've been summoned," Talon answers as a dark figure emerges from the shadows and a sense of unease gathers in my chest.

"What good work you've been doing here, Talon. The place practically reeks of death. But I'm afraid you haven't met your soul quota," the figure says coming into the dim light to reveal his devil horns.

"That's not possible, we've had a steady increase_—"

"Did I sound like I was finished talking?" the devil interrupts, and a chill slithers into the room. "You know the consequences of not delivering."

Silence answers him. We're all too aware that our time here could be stripped away at the snap of his fingers. Talon might run the place, but we all know who holds the deed.

"You only have a few more hours before time runs out, Talon. You really think you'll be able to deliver?"

Talon's back goes straight. "I'll kill every person in here if I have to." And I believe him.

"I need fifty more souls delivered by dawn, or this place gets ripped back to the fires of hell, and all your little monsters will belong to me."

A large bright fire consumes him where he stands, taking him back to where he came from.

We stand there looking down at the space he once occupied, knowing that this new proclamation changes things. Here I was thinking we could spend the rest of the night with our girl, but it looks like we'll be slaughtering the remaining souls that were unlucky enough to answer the call of this place.

"Is there not a loop-hole in the contract?" Matchbox asks, breaking the awkward silence.

Talon runs his hand through his dark hair. "I've gone over it a million times. There's no way we're short. I've been keeping count. We were ahead of schedule. This is the busiest we've ever been." He shakes his head in disbelief.

Nightmare Acres has been a haven for us monsters. A place

where we could exist, but with these rules wrapped around our neck, it isn't feeling as if we're truly free.

"How sure are you that we've met our quota?" I ask.

"I've gone over and over it, there's no way I made such a monumental mistake. I know the consequences."

"Well, then what if we just said fuck it?" Talon looks at me like I'm crazy.

"Hear me out, we continue on with the night like we have been, then when the devil comes back in the morning, we show him the evidence. And if he still insists that we're in breach of the contract, we fight him on it. There are hundreds of us here, we can take him."

"You're out of your mind."

"You have a better idea? We've spent years listening to that asshole's rules. Isn't it time we make our own?"

"There is one thing we could do," Talon says.

"What's that?" Matchbox asks.

"We need to get Olivia. And then maybe we'll have a chance."

"A chance for what?" I ask, as Talon opens the door below that leads outside.

"To save our fucking souls."

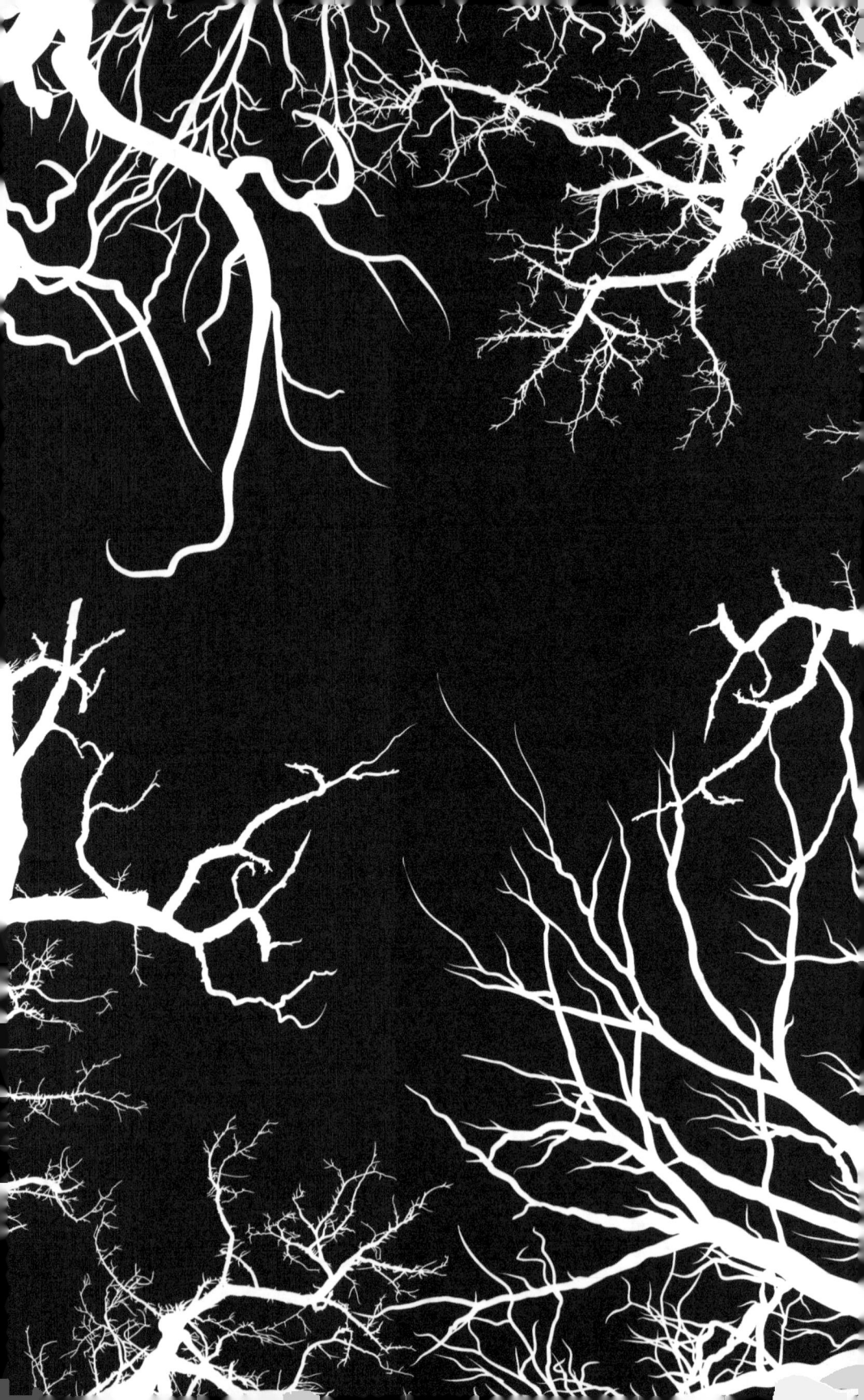

CHAPTER 12
OLIVIA

The hayride sways bumpily along the dark dirt road. Trees hang low as their bare branches brush against the tops of our heads. I'm secured tightly between two drunk guys dressed as *Dumb and Dumber* in their orange and blue tuxes while the haystack pokes uncomfortably at my bare legs. The smell of stale beer emanates from the guys' pores as they lean against me.

When I escaped from the haunted house, it spit me out at the beginnings of a corn maze, but to the right I saw they were loading up the hayride. Callie, Penny, and Shayla still are nowhere to be found, and my phone has no bars to try calling them. I did send a text asking where they were, but it's sitting in my messages showing as unsent. The hayride seemed like the more relaxing option — especially given how long I've been running tonight. It's already well past midnight, but the place is still packed.

"You here all by yourself, princess?" The one dressed in the blue tux asks.

"No, I'm just trying to find my friends."

"We can be your new friends," the one in pumpkin orange replies.

"That's okay, I'm just going to enjoy the ride."

A hand latches to my thigh and runs the length of my leg up to where the long shirt I'm wearing ends.

"We can help you enjoy the ride," his hot beer breath flutters against my ear and there's nowhere for me to go. If I jump off, I'll be lost in the woods, but if I stay, I'll have this nasty stranger's hands all over me. I'd rather cut off my own leg.

Suddenly, a deep roar comes from the dark tree line and the one who'd had his hands on me is ripped away faster than a blink of an eye.

"Oh shit—" the one in blue exclaims as he too is yanked off the hayride, disappearing into the mist.

The others on the ride are too engrossed in themselves to notice what's happened, but fear grips at my throat wondering if I'll be pulled off next.

When nothing happens for a moment, I think maybe I'm safe, but then the tractor comes to an abrupt stop, causing me to topple over on my hay bale.

"What the—" I utter, before finding myself being torn away from the hayride, and dragged over a strong pair of shoulders into the woods.

"Thought you could escape us so easily, did you?" Talon growls.

My ass is on full display, wind whipping against my backside as my shirt rides up, stuck between my body and his.

"Clearly not," I grumble, but inside my stomach is lurching into a somersault at having his hands on me again. "Where are you taking me?" My vision is limited to seeing his ass sway and the forrest floor. Moonlight cuts across the trees, casting ominous shadows along the path.

"You'll see," he answers, hands firmly holding me in place. Though, I don't miss the way his thumb rubs against my skin. Anticipation rolls around in my chest as I'm jostled about finally set down in a clearing. We're surrounded by trees on all sides, with a small bonfire lit in the center. My head swims having had all the blood rush to the top of my skull. It takes a moment for the world to stop spinning all around me. As it does, I note the two figures tied to two large poles sticking out of the ground. Each pole has firewood stacked at the bottom. If I didn't know any better, I'd say it looked like they were burning witches.

"Olivia," Talon says my name with such familiarity, like he's always rolled those syllables around on his tongue. It's a beautiful cadence, his voice. One that I wouldn't mind hearing forever.

"Please, have a seat," he gestures to a stump close to the fire. There are several situated in a semi-circle unoccupied and all at slightly varying heights. Smoke blows from the fire up into the air as it casts an orange hue to the space surrounding it. Though, I am grateful for the warmth licking across my bare legs as I settle into the seat.

Upon closer inspection, I note that both the men that have been tied up are also gagged. Unable to do anything but fight against their restraints. Their beady little eyes are full of fear.

"We have a proposition for you. One that will help us and

you, if you're interested," he says, hands locked behind his back, ever the image of a proper gentleman. It's a stark contrast to the wild woods that press in from all sides.

"I'm listening." I lean forward onto my knees, chin cupped in the palm of my hand and elbow propped up on my crossed legs. It's been a long night and the exhaustion is starting to creep in. Usually, I'd be long asleep by now. A yawn escapes my mouth making my eyes water.

"Something dire has been brought to our attention, and in order to keep this place running, we need to enact the loophole in the contract. You, are the key to that."

"ME?" I sit back stunned. "How? What contract."

Talon shuffles from foot to foot, clearly uncomfortable with having to ask for help.

"All of us signed a contract to be here. A deal with the devil, if you will. And as it stands, if we don't meet our quota, we lose this whole place. A piece of land we've all come to think of as home. A place where we can be free to be ourselves."

I finally ask the question that's been burning inside me since we rolled down the driveway. "This place, is it real?"

Talon drops his head nodding yes as he holds my gaze, waiting for my reaction. "So— the blood, the monsters, everything?"

"Everything."

Phantom and Matchbox emerge from the tree line, and I see it so clearly now. Matchbox with his gleaming horns and Phantom with his ethereal mist that clings to the edges of him. Talon's fangs catch in the firelight and my neck tingles remembering the way they pierced my tender skin. A part of me knew it, but the truth still feels like a bolder being dropped on my stomach.

"So— how can I help?"

"We need to perform a ritual that would bind you to the three of us. I never considered the possibility that a bind between different species of monsters and a human would be plausible. But tonight, has shown me that it could work. I know you've only just met us, and you owe us nothing. You could walk away from all this and forget tonight ever happened. Or, you can have a home here and belong to us," Talon says, walking closer to me until he's blocking my view of the fire. From this angle it looks as if the fire surrounds him.

I worry my bottom lip. There's no way I can even consider this. I have a life with my two daughters who I love more than anything. It might be a struggle, but it's mine.

"I don't think I can."

Talon's jaw ticks as he brings a finger up to tuck a rouge piece of hair behind my ear. "They would have a place here, Olivia. A life where they'd be provided for. Isobel and Jasmine would be protected and cared for."

"What kind of life could they have here? No, I can't. I couldn't do that to them."

"Well, if you don't then everyone human on the grounds will die," he responds. His demeanor is deathly still, conveying the seriousness of his words. "I won't sugarcoat it for you, little ghoul. You know what we are. What we're capable of. We are the creatures that ghost stories are made of. The monsters that haunt your nightmares. And we'll kill every single person here, including you, if it means we can keep our home."

"So, I don't have a choice then?" I ask, feeling frustrated

and exhausted. This whole night has been a series of what the fuck moments and I have no idea how to deal with any of it. I'm just a mom who was dragged out for a night of fun and ended up in a den of monsters.

"You have a choice, but we don't have a lot of time. So, either be with us, or don't," Talon snaps.

"What does it mean to be bound to you three?" I ask.

"Your soul would twine with ours. We'd be soulmates, therefore rendering the contract void. The devil crafted it in such a way thinking that the loophole would never come to pass. That I would never bind myself to a demon and a ghost, let alone a human. But tonight has shown me the error of my ways. The possibility of more that only you can grant us."

Heart racing and mind whirring, I watch as Phantom and Matchbox set the pyres alight. Could I really become soul bound with three creatures? They're murdering those men right before my eyes, and what scares me is I'm not even flinching.

"They touched you without permission, little ghoul. They deserve their fate," Phantom says, coming over to me smelling like smoke. I should be appalled that the guys from the hayride are about to be murdered in front of me, but a sick and selfish part of me feels honored.

"You would do that, for me?" I ask, dumbfounded. Trent wouldn't even take out the garbage for me, but these three have some guys tied up and lit on fire for daring to touch me. The thought makes me feel powerful. Cared for even in a twisted kind of way.

Fire reaches the men's boots, and they start to scream in

agony. A small smile forms on my lips and I know in that moment, there's no going back.

"Alright. I'll do it. But I need you to vow to never let any harm befall my girls. Swear it."

Talon grabs my hand and pulls me to standing, body pressed tightly against mine. "You have my word." He lowers his mouth to mine and seals my fate with a searing kiss.

The screams become background noise as I lose myself in the feel of Talon's lips on mine. His abs brush my stomach and I feel his ribs inhale as his strong hands grip into the roundness of my ass, grinding me up against his length.

Fuck, I need to feel him in me again.

My pussy is already drenched with the anticipation of what they're about to do to me.

Fangs pierce into my bottom lip as Talon sucks fat droplets of my blood into his wickedly handsome mouth. It's both pleasure and pain, making me clench the inner walls of my pussy, desperate to feel the fullness only these creatures can grant.

"Lay her out in the circle," Phantom says. Talon breaks the kiss and the fire burns brightly in his dark eyes.

"Are you ready?"

Truthfully, I haven't been ready for anything all night, but I nod my head yes anyway. He lifts me into his arms as if I weigh nothing, carrying me over to a crudely shaped circle made with twigs and leaves. Inside the circle is the shape of a pentagram laid out with large, gnarled branches. He sets me directly in the middle and produces a knife from his pocket. Each of the creatures kneel just outside the circle. Phantom, Talon, Matchbox, all ready to become bound with me. Distantly, I'm aware that the men have stopped screaming, finally succumbing to their tragic fate.

Talon opens up his pocketknife, the tip gleaming against the firelight.

"Give me your hand, Olivia," he commands, and I do, knowing that this choice will change me forever. But I'd rather live and still be there for my daughters, then become another claimed soul of Nightmare Acres.

He grips my hand in his, palm facing up and drags the tip of the knife against my flesh in a sharp diagonal cut. Blood bubbles up to the surface immediately, dripping down the sides of my hand and landing on my bare legs.

He does the same to his hand, Phantoms, and Matchbox's, then drops the knife in the dirt.

"Repeat after me, Olivia... With this blood, I thee bind."

"With this blood, I thee bind." A distant howl slices through the trees and the wind picks up swirling dead leaves all around us.

"And take my soul thus to twine."

"And take ... my soul... thus to twine." My muscles begin to shiver as the words come out of my mouth. It's almost too difficult for me to continue, but I push past the discomfort, eyes never leaving Talon's.

"Thrice entangled to their kind."

"And become forever mine," Talon finishes in unison with Phantom and Matchbox. He grasps my injured hand and pressing his open wound to my blood. Phantom and Matchbox each do the same and three thin invisible threads pierce my mortal heart.

I let out an agonizing scream as the sensation takes over my body and I fall to the ground.

CHAPTER 13
OLIVIA

I don't know how much time has passed, but when I open my eyes, my body feels different. Stronger. Made new.

Shaking my head, I rise from the circle, legs feeling like they're made of jelly. But when I finally stand at my full height, I note the three creatures that I'm now bound to, staring hungrily at me. The sensation of dirt and blood clings to my skin, but there's an underlying power running through my veins. I can feel my connection to them as much as I feel the breath in my own lungs. Vital, and wholly a part of me.

"How do you feel?" Phantom asks, eyes raking over my body. Everywhere his eyes scan, a tingling sensation erupts along my skin.

"Like I'm different somehow." I wiggle my fingertips trying to figure out what it is.

"That's because you've been infused with some of our essence, little ghoul. Becoming ours and only ours," Talon answers.

Looking down, I notice that the wound in my hand has closed as if it had never been there in the first place. Weird. I never know what the fuck is real here and what's fake. Did we even perform a ceremony or was it all in my head?

"You're not dreaming this up, little ghoul. It's really happening," Talon answers, reading my thoughts yet again. Invasive little prick.

He chuckles at that, and I feel my lips pull into a small smile.

"Come here," he commands, and I walk over to him heart thumping and skin aching to be touched. "You belong to us now, and we to you. That means even if you leave here, you can never be with anyone else. Only us."

"Only you," I agree, running my hand up his chiseled chest. I love the way it feels underneath my palms. So strong and defined. His dark brows raise as my hand continues its trajectory up and around to the back, letting my fingers wrap around the edges of his hair where it meets the nape of his neck. He is the very embodiment of danger, yet he regards me with care.

"So, you're a real-life vampire."

"Yes," he responds, hands gripping tight into the fleshy part of my waist. "At least now I get compared to that Damon guy instead of the sparkly one."

I let out a surprised laugh and regard him with fresh eyes. My vampire has a sense of humor hidden beneath all that rugged intensity.

"I never was much of an Edward girl myself," I reply.

"Is that right?" He leans down planting a soft kiss upon my lips. I take what he gives me greedily, drinking down the pleasure like a tonic for my weary and battered soul.

"Save some for the rest of us, Talon. I haven't even had a taste yet." Matchbox says, pulling at my arm and ripping me away from Talon's grasp.

Talon lets out a guttural animalistic growl that sends shivers down my spine.

"She belongs to all of us," Phantom says, putting himself between the vampire and the demon. Talon snarls in Phantom's face, but he doesn't flinch with the threat. Instead, he smirks and places his hand on Talon's chest, toying with him

Being fought over is something I'm not used to, and I think I rather enjoy it. Jealousy looks hot on them.

"Boys, please," I say, lifting the shirt off my body and discarding it into the dirt. They stop bickering immediately and swivel their attention to my naked body. "I'd like to be fucked thoroughly before the night is over."

"Happy to oblige," Matchbox says shoving Talon out of the way to get to me first.

If I'm not careful, these monsters might just tear me apart trying to claim me.

His hands are on me, and I tip my head back as he attacks my mouth with his. A low moan escapes my throat as he lifts me easily. Legs wrapping around his waist on instinct. There is a prominent bulge straining between his costume's fabric and my bare pussy. I ache to have it in me and find myself grinding on his cock as he lays me down in the dirt. Phantom isn't far behind already stroking his dick as he watches us. Matchbox discards his costume, revealing a toned physique covered in tattoos, piercings on both his nipples, and a barbel situated on the underside of his hard cock. My mouth waters thinking about how that will feel shoved inside me.

Talon glares down at us, the fire seemingly even more ablaze in those intense eyes of his.

"Come now. You agreed to share me equally, right? It's only fair," I chide at Talon's obvious jealousy. "Besides, I'm sure Phantom can entertain that big cock of yours while Matchbox fucks me." I bat my lashes at Talon teasingly.

"Fine," he grumbles. "But make no mistake, little ghoul. The three of us will fill all those tight holes of yours before the night is over." He threatens and it makes my pussy clench wondering what that might feel like. Having all three of them at once? I'm not sure I'd survive. But what a fun way to go out.

Matchbox lines his pierced cock up to my entrance as I lay back on my elbows, legs spread and waiting. He drags the tip through my wet slit before shoving his length in agonizingly slow. Inch by inch stretches me, and the cool metal scrapes against my insides in the most delicious pleasure. I need more.

Out of my periphery, I see Talon yank Phantom by the hair, positioning him in front of his hard dick, eyes never leaving me. "Is this what you wanted? To see us together?" he asks as he shoves his dick in Phantom's open and willing mouth.

Matchbox drives his cock into me finally reaching that perfect spot inside me and I groan out in pleasure. "Yes," I admit. Seeing the two of them together earlier had me in a puddle wondering what their relationship could be. The way they interacted with each other had me thinking it was new just like how they were with me. Tentatively exploring and enjoying what the others had to offer. All of us having some level of attraction to each other. I've never experienced this kind of dynamic before, but I can't say that I hate it.

His cock hits inside my core over and over again as he

fucks me right into the dirt. Clit rubbing against his pelvis, seeking that much needed friction to make myself come on him. I can already feel myself reaching that peak climax as he runs his rough calloused hands up my body, stopping at my breasts.

"These are fucking magnificent," he says, leaning down to take one of my nipples into his mouth while his hand kneads the flesh of my other breast. His fingertips linger on my pert nipple, twisting it slightly as he bites down on the one he's sucking on.

"Ow, oh holy fuck!" I yell, bucking my hips up even more as my eyelids flutter with the overwhelming sensation he's pulling from me.

"That's it, baby, fucking scream." He bites me again this time on the opposite nipple and another scream wrenches from my mouth as I come so hard, I see stars. He's not done yet though, twisting my body around so I'm lying face down in the dirt, ass up in the air. My tender breasts drag along the rough floor as Matchbox enters me once again. From this angle, he hits even deeper inside of me, and my fingers claw at the earth trying to accommodate his monstrous length that fills me to the brim.

It hurts so fucking good as I come on him again, this time feeling a squirt leak out of my stuffed pussy.

"Oh fuck," Talon groans, ripping Phantom off his cock and falling to his knees. Looking over my shoulder, I see him crawling to me. "I need to fucking taste it," he groans, leaning down and licking my juices from around my pussy as Matchbox continues to fuck me from behind.

Talon's hot mouth, licks both me and Matchbox as we fuck

and Matchbox's cock vibrates inside of me, growing even harder with each hot lick of Talon's mouth.

"Fuck you guys look so goddamn hot," Phantom says, stroking his cock. His mouth glistens with the evidence of Talon's come.

"Get over here," I demand, wanting to taste his cock in my mouth.

Phantom doesn't need to be told twice and scrambles over to me, positioning himself so that I can reach his hard dick. I lick his salty skin, feeling it pulsate beneath my tongue as Matchbox and Talon still work in tandem behind me.

I flatten my tongue and suck Phantom's dick right into my mouth, hollowing out my cheeks. His length is so considerable that I can only manage to get halfway down him before I start gagging.

"Relax that throat, little ghoul. You can swallow me down," Phantom says, gathering my hair in his fist and directing my head right where he wants me. My throat struggles against him as he pushes deeper in, hitting the back. His girth cuts off my access to oxygen and I feel a clawing desperation to breathe. Drool coats my chin as I gasp around him, feeling my pussy begin to stretch even more. It's clear that Talon has begun to press his cock in with Matchbox's and if I could scream, I would.

It fucking burns. I try to scramble away, because it's too much. Too fucking much, but they hold me in place. Right as black spots begin to fill my vision from the lack of air, Phantom releases me. I inhale greedy large gulps to the point of hiccuping before he shoves me down around him again.

"Come on, little ghoul. Swallow me down like you were made to."

I can hardly think as he fucks my mouth. The salty ribbons of come coat my mouth and I cough around him, face and throat covered with him.

Talon and Matchbox have managed to get their tips into me together and I wiggle back onto them. I'm stretched too much, but it's starting to feel like I could enjoy it. Their tips rub together inside of me as they push in and out.

"Fuck, I'm so close, Olivia. Look at how well you take us. Stretching so pretty for us," Matchbox says, digging his hands into my right hip as he presses farther in. I scream again as he forces me to stretch around the length of them both.

It's painful and yet they have me coming on their joined cocks, ripping the orgasm right out of me. My entire body shakes as I come this time and as I do, they release me from the joint hold and come all over my back in hot thick ribbons. Marking me as theirs.

Breathing hard, I can scarcely catch my breath, feeling like I've been beat up, but I fucking loved every second of it.

A distant howl breaks through the trees, bringing me back to the here and now. We're still at Nightmare Acres, just tucked away in a clearing.

"We need to move," Talon warns, and I catch the fear in his eyes.

What the fuck could scare a vampire? I wonder. The three of them hurriedly dress, throwing the discarded shirt at me. I follow their lead, wondering what the hell is going on, when what can only be described as a werewolf, bursts into the clearing, teeth bared and chest panting as if it has been chasing something.

"Run!" Talon commands, gripping me by the arm and pulling me with his vampire speed out of the way as the werewolf is joined by two others and headed right in our direction.

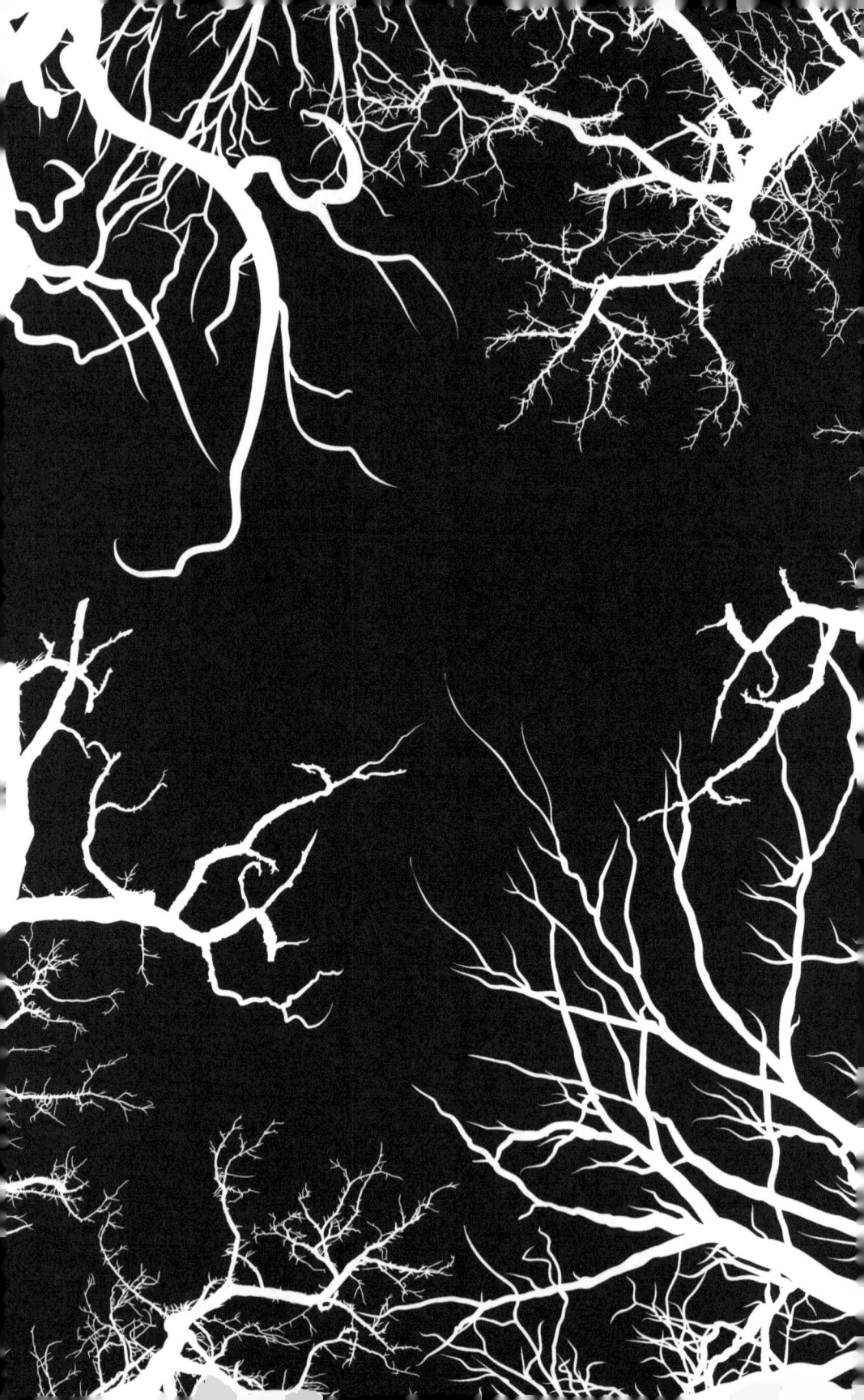

CHAPTER 14

MATCHBOX

T he wolves are hot on our heels, chasing us deeper into the woods. Howls reverberating off the trees, getting closer with each moment that passes.

"What the fuck? Aren't you in control of all the creatures here?" Olivia asks Talon as we make a dash for it.

"Not the werewolves," he answers, taking a sharp left. I realize he's headed to one of the summer cabins. A chance to shelter and grab weapons.

From what I know, the werewolves snubbed Talon's invitation to live amongst the monsters, choosing instead to hunt us, making the entire place their chosen nemesis. Feasting on anyone that was unlucky enough to cross their paths. No matter how many times Talon and his host of vampires had chased them off, they always came back. Picking apart our numbers for sport.

Legend is that the leader of the werewolves' pack had his mate killed by Talon, and from that point on they'd sworn to be the end of anyone associated with Talon. Meaning this place was at the top of their kill list, though it'd been weeks since there'd been a werewolf sighting. The full moon must have drawn them out.

"Through here," Talon commands, ducking into a graveyard. I haven't been this way before, and trip over one of the graves. The place is a mess of crumbling stones covered in moss and sinking into the soft earth. The graves look so old and decrepit that the names etched in are barely legible.

"Don't disturb the dirt here," Talon warns, slowing down to carefully guide us through, sidestepping a pile of leaves.

"Why not?" Olivia asks, gripping his arm and stumbling over her own bare feet. As she does, the ground shakes.

"Fuck. That's why," Talon says, pointing to a decaying hand emerging through the ground.

She looks down and sees the zombie pulling themselves out from the dirt, smelling rife with decay and moldy earth.

The werewolves spot us, and prowl into the graveyard, growling the closer they get.

"Now would be a great time to do something," Olivia says, eyes as wide as saucers.

"I got it." Grabbing the lighter in my pocket, I hurriedly light it between my fingers, throwing the flame at the pile of leaves. It goes up in a blaze of fire, licking across the dry ground, eating the dead foliage in seconds. The flames follow my command as it aims for the pack of werewolves, who snarl in defeat. Though one of the members seems to break away, jumping over the wall of fire I've created.

"Shit," Phantom declares, moving to intercept the threat. He disappears, using his stealth to attack the lone werewolf from the side. I can tell the moment Phantom collides with his body, as the werewolf swipes at the air, trying and failing to stop the invisible assailant. It gives Talon enough time to come in from the other side.

My flames hold steady, keeping the other werewolves at bay, but it's a temporary fix. I've expelled a lot of energy tonight, having spent most of it fucking my dream girl. I don't regret it for a second. It was the single hottest moment of my undead life.

Normally, I'd light the rest of the werewolves on fire, but experience has told me that would do more harm than good. They're already pissed at us but murdering more of their kind would bring down not just their pack, but others as well.

Olivia screams as one of the zombies grabs at her, bringing her into their grave. Her waist is halfway in the ground before I can get to her. As soon as I leave my post, the flames extinguish. A fact that the werewolves are quick to exploit.

They head straight at Talon, who thankfully transforms into his bat form just in time. Flying just out of their reach.

"Come on," I urge Olivia, seeing the cabin off in the distance. Phantom holds off the one werewolf, but I can't see where the other two went. She slides her small hand into mine while we make a run for it. Getting her to safety is my priority. I know that Talon and Phantom are more than capable of fending for themselves.

Just as we're about to get to the cabin door, one of the werewolves jumps out of the shadows, tackling Olivia to the ground.

"What's this?" they growl, sniffing at her face with their

long snout. Drool drops onto her face as she tries to get out of their grip.

"Get off her." I make to lunge at them, but they swipe out at me. Their strong muscular arm knocking me easily to the ground.

If my ribs aren't broken, they're most definitely bruised from the impact. Fuck, that hurts.

Blinking hard through the pain, I note there's a discarded axe over by a pile of chopped wood. If I can just make it there in time.

Spitting out a wad of blood from my mouth, I heave myself to standing and dash as quickly as my feet will carry me to where the axe sits embedded in a thick piece of wood.

"Killing you will bring my pack justice. A mate for a mate," the werewolf snarls, baring his teeth in Olivia's face. Tears stream down her beautiful, dirt-stained face.

Yanking the axe free, I barrel towards the creature, arms raised above my head. They won't take Olivia. I won't let them.

Just as the werewolf is about to close its large maw down on Olivia's neck, I bring the sharp tip of the blade down onto its neck. Severing muscle and bone from its body. Blood sprays out, gushing all down Olivia's body. I must have hit an artery.

The werewolf's body collapses on top of Olivia, trapping her beneath the enormous fur ball. She shoves at the corpse with all her might, trembling and covered in warm, sticky blood. I help move it off her, pulling her out from beneath.

Killing the werewolf will bring repercussions, but if I hadn't then Olivia would be dead.

"Thank you," she says, looking up at me with heavy lashes.

I feel a smirk forming along my lips. "It was nothing."

"Oh yeah? So, I shouldn't give you a thank you kiss?"

"I'm not saying that." I lean to take her mouth in mine, but as I'm about to plant a kiss on her, a low agonizing howl comes from where the fallen werewolf's body is. Turning, I see the other two werewolves.

Olivia yanks the axe out of the corpses's neck and raises it. "You want to be next?" She asks with a deadly chill to her voice.

"Enough blood has been spilt of my kind tonight. Mark my words, you haven't seen the last of us." The werewolf on the left says before they take off into the night.

Olivia drops the axe and breathes a sigh of relief.

"Where are Talon and Phantom?" she asks.

"Right here," Talon answers as Phantom shimmers into his corporeal body.

It's clear one of the werewolves took a swipe at Phantom, seeing three large slices in his arm. Olivia runs to him and tries to stop the bleeding.

"Are you alright?" Talon asks, rubbing the blood from her dirtied face.

She nods.

From the position of the moon, I can tell we don't have much longer with our little ghoul.

"How about we play one more game before the night ends?" Talon asks.

"What game is that?"

"Our favorite. Hide and seek," Phantom answers, injury forgotten. It looks superficial anyway.

"What about the werewolves?" Olivia asks, worrying her bottom lip.

"We don't have to worry about them anymore. At least not

tonight." I say, knowing they'll eventually be back. "But if you're worried, I can bring the axe."

She nods her head.

"Now, go hide from us. And when we catch you, we'll fuck your brains out." Talon says, fangs gleaming in the moonlight.

She takes off running into the dark, and we start counting, ready to catch her one last time.

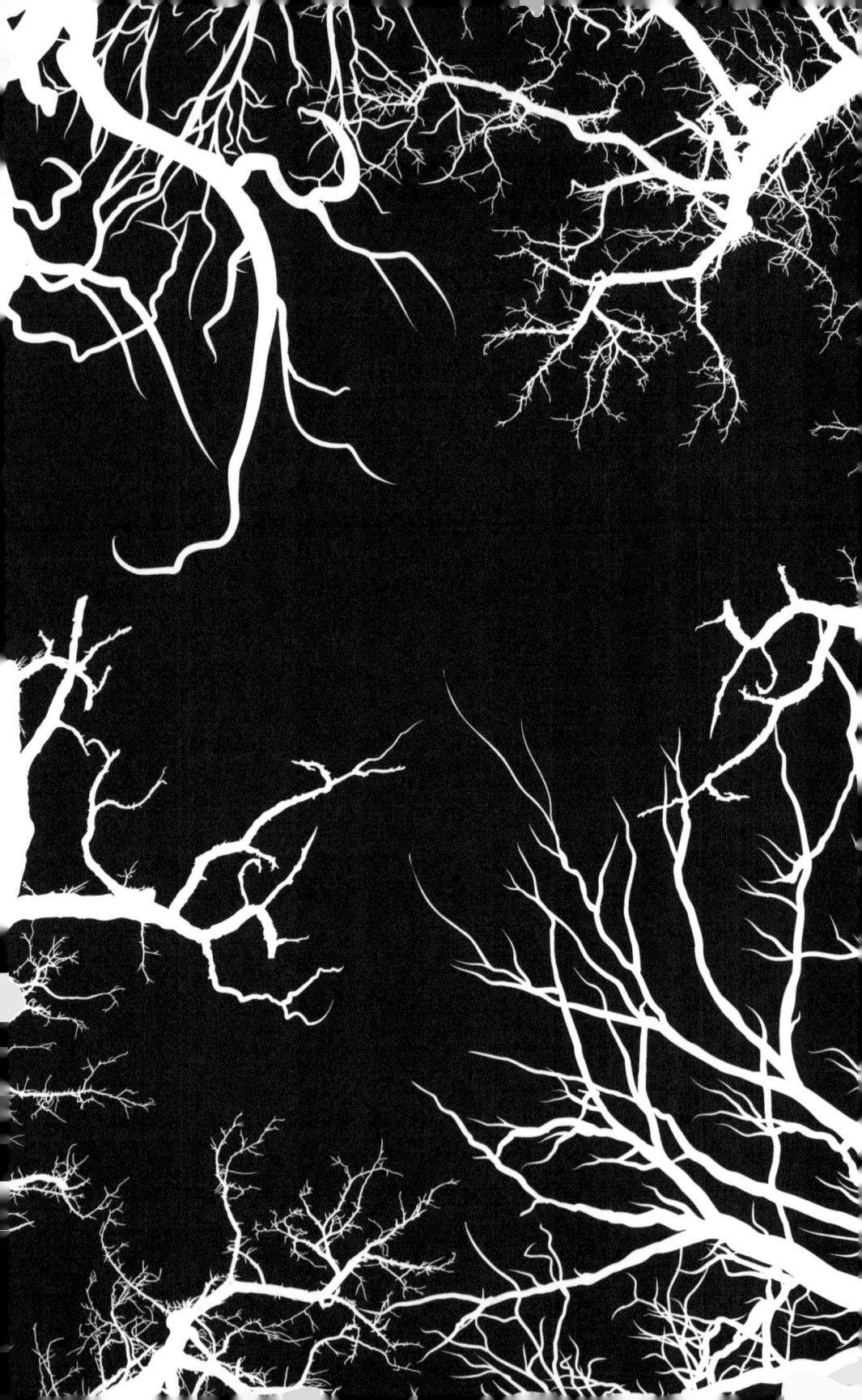

CHAPTER 15

TALON

Breathing in the cool night air, I roll my shoulders. Ready to seek out my prey like the primal hunter I am.

The attack from the werewolves threw me. Normally, they stick to the outskirts, picking off any stragglers. I don't know what emboldened them to get so close this time. The thought unsettles me. They've always been a nuisance, but if they're stepping up their game, I'll need to be more prepared. At least, I think that's the last we'll see of the tonight. They don't take loss well.

Cracking my knuckles, I wait as the time ticks by, giving Olivia ample time to hide from us. Though, I can sense she's not far.

Tonight, has been nothing but surprises for me, and that's saying something. Not much can surprise a thousand year old vampire, but tonight is an exception. I'd never anticipated binding myself to a human, but Olivia is not just any human.

She has a spark about her. A lightness that's yearning to be set free.

I know our time is limited which is why I want to force to play these games with us. Pushing her to embrace this side of herself that she didn't know she had until tonight. It's been mesmerizing seeing her come alive.

As we count down, the ground beneath our feet rumbles.

"Fuck," I growl, knowing exactly what that means. Or rather who it means is here.

"What the hell have you done?" the devil exclaims, towering over me.

"I broke the contract," I say, void of any emotion.

His face pulls into a snarl as he looms over me. "We are not finished. You might have found a loophole tonight, but I will have my souls."

"We fulfilled our end of the deal, devil. We're done here."

"For now," he says. "One day soon, you will need me again. Monsters can only stay hidden for so long."

He leaves in a plume of smoke and sulfur, and a vaguely veiled threat that I know better than to take lightly. When you dance with the devil, you're bounded to get burned. But make a deal with one? Might as well set the whole world on fire.

"Fuck this. I'm going to find Olivia," Matchbox says.

I can't agree more.

We take off hunting for where she might have hidden. Knowing the most obvious path she must have taken is headed back to where the main house sits. Though the grounds here are expansive, she's probably wanting to link up with those friends of hers that brought her here. We haven't stumbled upon them once all night.

A rustling off in the distance catches my attention. Most animals steer clear of this place, knowing the danger that lurks within. The rustling happens again, and I fade towards it in record speed. Sure enough, Olivia is attempting to crouch behind a bush.

She's a vision covered in dirt, blood, and our collective come. Blonde hair looking matted but no less gorgeous. I actually prefer her better like this. She looks like a survivor. Strong and unbending, and wholly mine. Well, ours, but Phantom and Matchbox are still a ways off in the woods. I have her all to myself.

I creep soundlessly until I'm right on top of her, tackling her to the ground with my hands around her slim throat.

"Found you," I say, squeezing ever so tightly. She looks up at me in this upside-down position. I can see down the length of her body. The evidence of the night staining her legs with bruises and scrapes. Marring her perfect skin with the memories of us.

My cock is already hard and needing release. I'll never tire of her, that much I know.

"Now take my cock out and suck, little ghoul. Suck like your fucking life depends on it." Her pulse flutters beneath my fingertips as she unzips me and takes my fat, heavy cock out. A bead of pre-cum falls on her plump lips, and she licks them on instinct. I smirk, knowing just what dirty thoughts swirl in that pretty head of hers. She wants this. No— craves it.

I angle my hips above her and feed my cock into her open mouth as I squeeze her throat.

"Fuck, that feels so good," I murmur, pulsing down into her

as she licks my length and gags around my cock. The vibrations in her throat feel so fucking good.

"What do we have here?" Phantom asks, finding us easily. Matchbox isn't far behind, standing with his arms crossed.

"Too late, fuckers. Winner gets the reward."

"Fuck that, she's ours just as much as yours, Talon. Stop being a possessive old bastard," Matchbox says, undoing his pants.

He pins her hips down, and pries open her legs.

With one thrust he enters her, pierced cock rutting up into that tight as fuck pussy. She moans around my length, and I feel my balls squeeze with the need to release.

Before I know it, I'm coming down her throat, which she sucks down. Every single drop.

"You're getting better at that," I say, pulling myself out and wiping her mouth. Within a few more pulses, Matchbox has her coming around his cock, her fingernails digging into his back as he spills his seed into her.

She's on birth control and takes it regularly from what I can see in her mind, so there's no worry of cross breeding with her tonight. And I don't think that's something she wants. She's already had two perfect babies that she dotes on. From the way she thinks about them, I can tell she's a wonderful mom. Another fact about her that makes her even more attractive to me. So many people only care about themselves, but Olivia cares so much for everyone else, with no one to care about her.

"We caught you so quickly, little ghoul," Phantom says, with a kiss on her swollen lips. I know he can taste me there, and it makes my dick twitch. "Run for me. One more time."

She smiles, taking off, and this time into the corn maze.

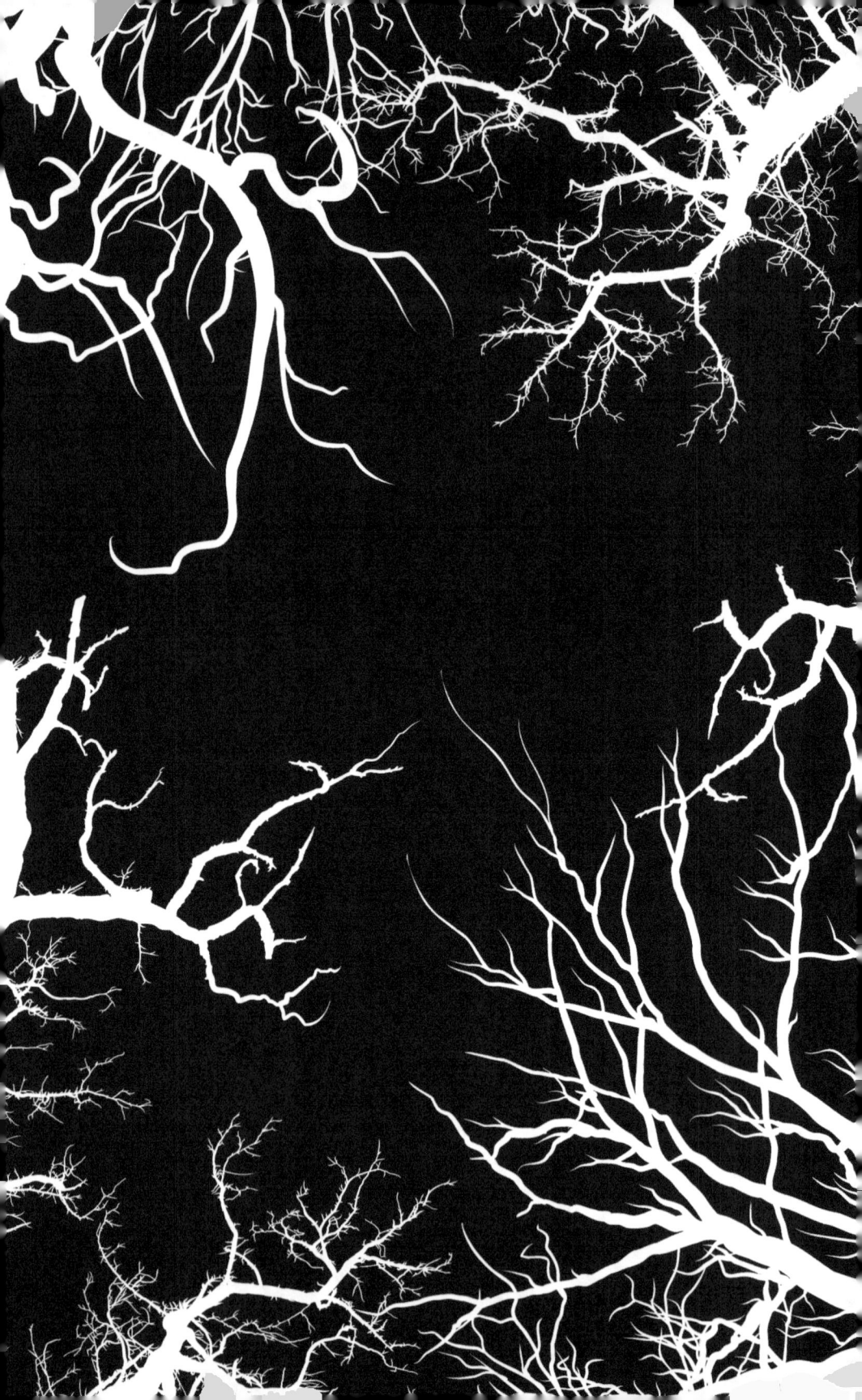

CHAPTER 16
OLIVIA

The taste of Talon on my tongue lingers, and my pussy aches with each step. I wonder how Callie, Shayla, and Penny are doing as my feet brush against the dirt. A distant howl breaks my thoughts, and fear takes over my senses again. I'd barely escaped that werewolf earlier, and now they'e back, with my creatures nowhere to be found. I pick up my pace, trying to decipher which way to go at a crossroads. Heavy steps come from what sounds like every direction. They're close.

Shit.

I take a left, picking up my pace, though my body protests.

The moonlight cuts across the field of decaying corn husks that crackle with each burst of howling wind. I can scarcely differentiate between the howls of the roaming beasts, and the ones coming from the windy weather. It all blends into a symphony of terror. My chest is tight from running through the endless labyrinth. I'm being hunted. Corralled to who knows where.

Exhaustion burrows deep into my bones, but I have to keep moving.

The uneven ground and minimal light make it difficult to see where I'm stepping. The hole swallows my foot and twists my ankle before I have a chance to realize what happened, I'm face down in the dirt, wind knocked out of my chest and hands smarting from the hard impact. Corn swishes next to me in the breeze as I groan out in pain.

A low growl alerts me to the predator before I'm yanked back into the corn by a roughly calloused hand.

"Shhh," Matchbox urges and I listen, letting him tuck me against his large body. The obsidian-colored horns on his head shimmer in the moonlight, though we're mostly covered down in the shadows. He rubs my chilled skin, warming me up. I note he still has hold of the axe from earlier, and that makes me feel marginally better knowing we can defend ourselves if we need to.

With these creatures I've met tonight, I feel completely safe around them, which is insane. They're killers. But I know they'd never hurt me. Instead, they make me feel worshipped. I fucking love it. I love them for it.

Ears straining, I listen intently as a high-pitched whine echoes around us, followed by whimpering and finally a scurrying of paws passing our hiding place.

"It's alright I got the last of them," Talon promises, leaning down to offer me a hand. I take it, feeling the coolness of his skin wrap around me as he pulls me to standing.

"That was fucking close," I murmur. He takes me into his arms, wrapping himself around me in a protective hug.

"I would never let anything happen to you," he promises, kissing me on the top of my head.

"Are you hurt?" I ask, as he rubs a small circle on my lower back.

He chuckles, "It takes a lot to harm me. I'm fine I swear it. Are you well?" He looks down the length of my body for any injuries, but I shrug him off.

"I'm fine."

A riot of familiar laughter comes from behind one of the stalks of corn, and I whip my head in the direction.

"Callie?" I ask, following the sound.

I'd know that laugh anywhere, having heard it since we were little. I chase after her.

"Callie is that you?"

As I round the corner, I wish I'd stayed back. The sight that greats me is one that I could never have imagined in a million years. Shock reverberated through my entire body as I see Trent wrapped around Callie in an intimate embrace, with his tongue down her throat.

Heart hammering in my ears, I gape at the betrayal unfolding before my very eyes.

"Trent?" I stare unbelieving at my ex with his arm wrapped around my best friend's waist. "Where are the girls?"

Panic, more than I've felt this whole night, drops deep into my stomach as a million scenarios flit through my mind. It's clear Callie didn't expect to be caught, because she tries to shrug off Trent's slimy embrace, to no avail.

"Relax. They're fine."

Talon comes up behind me, arms crossed and fangs lengthening, cocks his head as a deadly stillness takes over his body. "She asked you a question."

"The fuck buddy, leave us alone, we're having a conversation."

Callie shuffles uncomfortably on her feet as her eyes bounce from person to person. I wish I could grab her by the shoulders and shake her, making her answer why the hell she would betray me like this. After all we have been through and how she's seen first-hand how cruel Trent can be. But what really snags my attention is the fury gathering from the men that have been ravaging me all night.

Talon, Phantom, and Matchbox are all honed in on my ex and the air crackles with imminent danger. Trent, however, seems utterly oblivious as usual. I've always thought his pride would be his downfall, and with the way these men are looking at him, I'm about to be proven right.

"The girls, Trent. Where. Are. They?" I grit out as anger like I've never known ignites deep inside my chest cavity. I feel downright murderous.

"Would you calm down, alright? They're with that neighbor of yours. Mrs. Hannibal. You weren't home, so what was I supposed to do?"

"Hannigan, you imbecile! Her name is Mrs. Hannigan. And you could have, I don't know, actually taken them out trick or treating like you said you would instead of ditching them for some hot piece of ass, again." I'm done with niceties. Done being a doormat for this waste of space and too hurt by my supposed best friend to even look at her. I've had enough and need to know that my daughters are safe. My fingers grip my phone that displays a prominent new crack across the screen as I dial up my neighbor thanking the stars that I have a fucking signal. Each ring of the dial tone feels like an eternity. Finally, on the fifth ring, she answers, sounding like I've woken her.

"Hi, Mrs. Hannigan, I'm so sorry to wake you, but are the girls there? This is Olivia." My words sound rushed to my ears as I wait for her reply.

A shuffling noise fills the earpiece and then, "Oh, yes. That sperm donor of theirs came by earlier tonight. Said he had some sort of emergency, and you were out. They're asleep now, don't worry."

Relief rushes through me and I want to crumple into the floor. "Thank you. I'll be there soon."

"No rush. They're sleeping so soundly. Besides, with how hard you work, you deserve a night off for once." Tears sting at my eyes.

"Thank you." We hang up and I feel a rush of gratitude that we are lucky enough to have a Mrs. Hannigan in our lives. The girls love her to pieces, and she's become like an adopted grandma to the girls since my own parents have long since passed, and Trent's parents are just as absent as their deadbeat son.

A strong hand finds its way to my lower back rubbing a small comforting circle as I calm myself down enough to face my ex, who has the nerve to be nuzzling against Callie's throat.

"You've got to be kidding me," I practically growl as the anger rises. I'm vibrating with it, feeling the pure white-hot rage from years of disappointments and countless hours of frustrations. Is this what my children have to look forward to?

A lifetime of being saddled with a man who can't even manage to spend a few hours with them?

No.

No more.

They deserve more than that, and so do I.

I don't even realize the moment my fingers clutch around the axe sitting in Matchbox's grip, but there they are yanking it away from him. And almost like I'm seeing myself from afar, I watch in horror, and a small amount of awe, as I see my body take a swing at my ex, lodging the weapon directly in his spine.

The noise he makes is inhumane.

He crumples as Callie runs off screaming, only to be grabbed and restrained by Phantom.

"Let me go! What the hell, Olivia?" Callie screams, but I ignore her, stepping around the body of my ex as he struggles for breath.

Blood bubbles out of Trent's mouth and slides down his stubbled chin. The axe sits lodged in his skin so deep, I know it hit bone. It takes a great amount of strength to wrench it out of him and when I do, I see my hands bloodstained and shaking. But as I look down at him, glassy eyed and covered in his blood, I don't feel a hint of remorse.

"Wait," He croaks out, but I'm done listening. Done with his plethora of excuses that never can make up for what he's put us through.

"Fuck you, Trent."

The blade to the axe comes down on his neck, slicing cleanly through his jugular and ending him on the spot. I pour every hurt into my arms with a scream upon my lips for all the hurt he's caused me. The axe grinds through all the layers of bone and muscle until finally, his head is completely removed from his body in a spectacular mess of blood and rage.

I fall to my knees next to his lifeless body and take his hand in mine.

"I'm sorry, but that's just the way it has to be," I whisper to him, as if he can still hear me. None of this feels real, but deep down I know that it is, and I've just taken my girls father from them. I hope that they can forgive me. I hope they can see that I did it for them. So they won't have to grow up accepting that kind of treatment from someone who is supposed to love them unconditionally, not just whenever it's convenient for them. Come to think of it, I don't think Trent ever really loved the girls, or me. He just used us. We were nothing but building blocks to him on his way to the life he thought he deserved.

Only now that life will be buried six feet deep.

Standing, the axe feels heavy in my hands. I twirl it around like a cheerleader with a baton sending a splattering of Trent's blood in the air.

"You know, Callie, I trusted you," I start off, watching her squirm against Phantom's hold. "You've seen how he's treated me and the girls." I shake my head with disbelief —tears stinging at my eyes.

Memories of our friendship flit like a video montage in my brain wondering how long she's been fucking him.

"I expect this kind of shit from Trent, but not from you. Why, Callie?"

She doesn't answer, but instead looks at me with no emotion emanating from her perfectly made-up face, jaw shut tight around her crimson painted lips. Her dyed black hair looks almost blue in the moonlight, and I feel in that moment my heart begins to crack at what I thought was a lifelong friendship turning to dust before me. This level of betrayal that I never thought possible has rendered me murderous and unrecognizable. Before I came to this place, I only thought that I could take a life under the most dire of circumstances, such as saving my kids. But after the night I've had being tormented and pleasured by real life monsters, a part of me has been awakened. Capable of an evil that should frighten me.

"Don't beat yourself up, Olivia," Talon's voice soothes. "What's Halloween without a little murder, mayhem, and madness?"

A smile curls around my mouth. "You're right," I peck Talon on the cheek and a deeply guttural animalistic sound rumbles from his chest.

"That's my little ghoul. Now make her bleed, I'm feeling rather hungry."

"You wouldn't," Callie scoffs.

She's right. The Olivia she thinks she knows wouldn't, but the person I've become tonight absolutely would. I know what she sees when she looks at me. Meek, mild-tempered, Olivia. Go-with-the-flow, Olivia. The same girl I've been since we met in kindergarten. Always bending to Callie's will and doing whatever she thinks is best.

"No?" I taunt, spinning the axe around as I stalk closer to her. "You watched that man," I point at Trent's lifeless bludgeoned body with the tip of my axe, "make my life hell for years, and you stood by my side acting like you were being supportive. Acting like my friend. But friends don't do that to each other."

She settles me with a stare I've seen one too many times.

It's the one she reserves for people she thinks she's outwitted. "Who do you think told him about the cats peeing in Isobel's crib?"

My stomach plummets to my feet. When Trent and I were in court he accused me of having the cats pee in our daughter's crib as a litter box. Which they'd only done once, and I'd went and purchased a brand-new mattress for Isobel with the little money I'd had saved. Though at the time, the judge was too keen to believe Trent's version of the story, making me take parenting classes while Trent walked away Scott free.

That story was nothing but a twist of the truth that caused myself and my girls' immense amounts of pain having the court think I was somehow neglectful. I'd cried on Callie's shoulder that night, shaking with anger at how unjust the justice system could be, and the whole time it came from her? A wolf in sheep's clothing that I had let burrow into my life, trusting with my secrets and my children. They call her Aunt Callie for Christ's sake.

"Want me to light her on fire?" Matchbox offers, and a flicker of fear jolts across Callie's face. Good. She should be afraid, because if she thought what I did to Trent was bad, she has no idea how terrible it could be. Trent's death was quick. Nearly painless.

"Yeah, you know what? Burn that bitch to the ground. But make it slow."

"WHAT?" Callie screeches, but it's too late, flames lick the bottoms of her boots causing her to start screaming and kicking. Phantom's grip holds tight as he allows his bottom half to turn into his ghost form, making it so that Callie's still being held in place. She kicks uselessly at the flames, but they only crawl up higher, wrapping around her like a golden snake.

"Stop! Stop this please! Olivia, I'm s-sorry. I shouldn't have- AHHHHH, Fuck! It hurts! Please, stop!"

I tilt my head to the side taking in the sight of my former best-friend flailing about and begging for mercy. Pathetic.

The scent of her charred skin wafts through the air making me scrunch up my nose. I should be feeling a twinge of regret right now. An ounce of remorse or guilt. But in the space where those emotions should inhabit is a big fat expanse of apathy.

"Olivia! Fuck please, you're my best-friend. I'm sorry, I fucked up! Ahhhh! Fucking stop this you cunt!"

The flames crawl higher, wrapping around her waist and causing her to writhe in pain.

"Drop her, Phantom. I want to see the look in her eyes when I take her life," I say raising the axe above my head, held tightly in both of my hands.

Callie plops to the ground in a heap of burnt flesh and painful sobs. The flames extinguish upon impact, but smoke still emanates from her ruined legs.

"Since we're not really friends like I thought, you won't mind if I just finish what I started," I say looking down at her. My arms come down hard and lodge the edge of the blade straight into her neck. A gurgle of blood sprays out from her mouth and her open wound, as her life ends with one abrupt hit, severing her head completely. I marvel at my newfound strength in disbelief as Talon steps over and grabs two finger-fulls of her blood, sucking them into his mouth as he wraps his hand around my calf. My chest rises and falls with an immense amount of labor as I marvel at all the gore.

"Fucking delicious," he moans, leaning down to suck her dry. And he does. Her body is devoid of any blood in a matter of moments as Talon feasts from her corpse.

He stands, blood dripping from his handsome face as he leans down to take my mouth in his.

"Taste what you've done, my murderous little ghoul," he demands closing his mouth onto mine. The metallic tang invades my tastebuds immediately as he languishes his tongue against mine in a heady, passionate kiss. My adrenaline is still pumping through my veins as I let Talon explore my mouth, relishing in the feel of him against me. My monster.

All of them feel like mine. These creatures I've stumbled upon in this cursed place. Forever altering my life as I know it. I came here afraid. A shrinking violet in a world built to crush my delicate petals, but I came out forged in fires of hell. Strong as iron and unashamed of my choices. Though, I'm admittedly shocked by my actions, I guess we all have that breaking point, and this was mine.

Giving into the feel of Talon, I embrace my newfound boldness breaking the kiss and exposing my neck to him. "Bite me, please," I beg, wanting to feel everything he has to offer me.

He groans, and I watch as his fangs lengthen. "Such a beautiful little temptress. Offering yourself up like my own personal sacrifice." His fangs drift over that sensitive area on my neck, hovering ever so lightly above my pulsating jugular. He pierces my skin gently. Like a pinprick. But the sensation it brings is delectable.

"Woah, dude, look at that charred bitch. So fucking lifelike. It even smells fucking burnt." We break apart as a few stragglers burst through the corn maze. I can feel small drops of blood sliding down my neck as they pass us by, hardly paying us any attention in their meandering state.

The sound of a chainsaw whirs to life behind them as the spotlight drags over the tips of the corn, illuminating the gruesome scene before us.

Trent's and Callie's severed heads have rolled together, and their bodies lay haphazardly strewn across the dirt path.

"This place is so fucking cool," one of them chuckles, kicking Trent's head like a goddamn soccer ball into the corn field. I can't help but let out a giggle seeing the way it wobbled.

The chainsaw wielding performer slices through the cornstalks, head tilted and covered in blood. The guys make no move to run, and I can tell it's a deadly mistake. He lifts the device over his head, saw churning a million miles a minute before bringing it down on one of the guy's arms.

"Oh fuck!" his friend screams, but it's too late. There's no escape now. The chainsaw rips into his chest, slicing him in half. The sounds of maniacal laughter mix with the raging roar of the chainsaw as he finishes off the group.

"That's enough, Bloodbath," Talon says, and the command works. Bloodbath cuts the engine to the chainsaw and hoists it over his shoulder, carrying it like a sack of potatoes. The bodies lay in a mess of missing limbs and blood, but it's the cresting of the dawn that catches my eye. And the signal that the night is coming to an end.

CHAPTER 17

PHANTOM

My murderous little ghoul looks so gloriously seductive covered in the blood of her worthless ex. Watching her kill him so ruthlessly got my dick so fucking hard. I could strip her down and fuck her senseless right here for how proud I am of her.

The moment that douchebag's soul left his body, I felt the ground shake with the absorption of his energy, fueling the lifeblood of this wicked place. And adding her best friend to the evening's body count solidifies that this woman was made for us.

What started as a mere indulgence is now a fully-fledged obsession- a deep soul-crushing need to keep her for ourselves. She's a queen amongst monsters. A vision of beauty splattered in blood, sweat, and come. We don't deserve her but fuck if that's going stop us from trying.

The sun is rising, meaning we need to get Talon and the other vampires inside, and fast.

"We need to go," Talon says looking at the looming horizon, shifting immediately into his bat form.

Olivia crouches down to her friend's corpse and rummages in her jacket pocket before producing a set of keys. The night is ending and with it the knowledge that we might never see Olivia after she leaves this place. That thought burns deep in my gut. Though we're bound, she has no obligation to come back to us.

Light flickers along the fine mist as we make a dash for the edge of the corn maze. We're close and might just make it to the doors in time. From my vantage point, I can see that Talon has already ducked inside taking shelter from his one weakness. The sun.

I grip her hand in mine as I pull her along the maze. I know the layout like the back of my hand and have her safely at the end of it in no time.

"Wait," She gasps for breath, holding her side with her free hand as she yanks on me to slow down.

"Olivia, we're creatures of the night, we have to get the vampires inside," I explain, tugging at her to follow me.

"I have to go, Phantom. My girls they need me, and I've been gone too long."

I knew this was coming. Knew that it was too good to be true, and that she'd leave us eventually.

"Thank you, for saving us." I say not wanting her to go, but with the dawn's light fast approaching, we're out of time.

"I don't want to leave, but I have to. I love my girls more than anything, Phantom, and they need me. Especially now that their dad will never be coming back to them."

Nodding my head, I give her one last kiss. It's short and sweet, and filled with the salty taste of her tears.

"Go," I command, retreating to the safety of the house where Talon and Matchbox wait in the doorway.

The three of us watch as she makes her way to her friend's car. As she goes, her blonde hair catches in the sun making her look like the goddamn angel she is. Just as she's about to open the door, she looks back at us with a sad smile as she waves. The three of us wave back, saying goodbye to the woman who owns each of our hearts. She pulls out of the parking lot slowly, and we watch as she drives right out of our lives, possibly forever.

OLIVIA

ONE YEAR LATER: HALLOWEEN

Isobel and Jasmine run around dressed as ghosts. They've each donned a white sheet with cut out holes for the eyes. Though, Jasmine has added a flower crown to her ensemble saying it makes her look "chic". A word she fully mispronounces in the cutest way. I let it slide, wanting her to stay little awhile longer.

It's been one year since I bound myself to the three creatures that rule my heart, and just as long since I'd dared to step on the grounds. But that all changes tonight.

The last three hundred and sixty-five days I've spent building my life into one that I can be proud of. I quit the gas station and have been working on obtaining a degree in business, working on graphic design to pay the bills. Something I always wanted to do, but had Trent's voice of doubt always stopping me. Trent was declared a missing person, and his minimal estate was gifted to the girls, allowing us to afford groceries for once.

As for Callie, well, her body was found mangled on the side of the road and her family had a service for her that I chose not to go to. Apparently, Penny and Shayla had made it off the grounds that night, hitching a ride with another couple they'd met in the haunted house.

They were lucky to escape.

I pull out my phone and type in the search bar, finding exactly what I'm looking for. The video begins to play, showing the familiar entrance to the place I've been too much of a coward to go back to. Even if it's broken my heart not to. "Come to Nightmare Acres, for a Hallows Eve fright." An ominous voice taunts from my speakers as the frame pans over to the Haunted House, showing people running with shirts that have "I survived Nightmare Acres" splayed across the front. My cheek twitches remembering that night a year ago. Maybe I'm crazy for wanting to go back.

"Okay, girls. Have fun tonight. I'll see you in the morning. Come give Mommy a hug," I say as the two most adorable ghosts come running into my arms, linking their small limbs around my neck.

"I love you, Mommy," They say at the same time.

"Listen to Mrs. Hannigan," I say, watching them walk out the door with our trusty neighbor.

"Have fun tonight," Mrs. Hannigan replies.

"I plan to," I respond, keys in hand and a bounce in my step.

The drive to the grounds seems to take forever, but finally, I 'm turning down the familiar dirt road. It looks the same, like no time has past.

A flutter of nervousness churns in my stomach. What if they don't remember me. Or worse, they do, and they want nothing to do with me.

I bring the car to a stop, parking in the last empty spot. It's even busier than last year and looks ten times as intense. There are performers jumping around and people screaming already, and I haven't even gotten past the entrance yet.

As soon as I shut my car door, I feel them. A shift in the air raises the small hairs on the back of my neck, and as I turn, I see them in the distance. All three looking at me with such intensity, I know in my gut that what I experienced last year at this same place wasn't a fluke. It was real, and what we have together is real.

I walk with purpose towards them, ignoring the revelry that surrounds me, and instead hold the gaze of the three creatures that rule my heart and soul.

"Hey," I say, feeling the nerves take over.

"It's been a year and you open with hey?" Matchbox spits out.

Unease fills my chest. Maybe this was a bad idea. It's been too long.

"Shut up, Matchbox," Talon says, stepping forward and tucking my hair behind my ear. "I like your haircut." He says leaning down and smelling my neck.

"Th-thank you."

"Mmm still the same little ghoul I remember," he groans, licking my sensitive skin and raking his fangs against my flesh. I shudder, remembering how good they all felt all too well.

"We've missed you," Phantom says, taking me into his

grasp. I let him pull me into a hug, feeling every defined muscle press against my front.

"Fine, yes. We missed you," Matchbox admits and I let out a chuckle.

"Actually, I only came to get my missing *Sleeptoken* hoodie I lost last year," I joke.

"The only name I want to see splayed across those tits, are one of ours," Talon says, smacking me on the ass and making me shriek with delight.

These creatures, these monsters, feel more like home to me than Trent ever did. Accepting me for who I am and making me better that who I was.

"Why don't we get reacquainted by taking a stroll through the haunted house?" Phantom suggests, grabbing my hand and pulling me along.

"Lead the way," I say, following them into the place that started it all—into the dark and surrounded by echoing screams.

Want more from Nightmare Acres?
Be sure to preorder the sequel here.

ACKNOWLEDGMENTS

Thank you, the reader, first of all for picking up my spooky little book. This was so much fun to write, and I'm so grateful that you've chosen my book to read out of all the options you have.

To my husband, thank you for forcing me to watch scary movies. How far we've come from our first date when you took me to see the movie, *Mama*. Could you ever have predicted that one day I'd be writing erotic horror? I couldn't. I didn't even watch the movie on our date, instead I hid behind my hands, too scared to even look at the screen. That girl would never believe I write what I do now. So, thank you for expanding my horizons. I can even watch some scary movies now! Though, I refuse to watch *The Ring*. It's not happening.

Thank you to Melissa for offering to read this and giving me feedback when I was on such a tight time crunch.

Thank you to my other Melissa for being my solid rock, who's been with me all these years. Supporting my nonsense and listening to all my mundane daily wins and complaints. I love you, girl.

PLAYLIST

Scream by Once Monsters

Freak Show by Punkinloveee, H3artcrush

Come 2 Me by Jonny Goth

Blood In The Cut by K. Flay

Dragula (from "Haunt") by Lissie

MONSTERS by Shinedown

Heads Will Roll by Yeah Yeah Yeahs

Kill Of The Night by Gin Wigmore

HELP by Isabel LaRosa

ALSO BY DAKOTA WILDE

Kildale Academy Series

Hell House

Hell House Halloween

Queens of Hell House

Reign of Hell House

Standalones

My Teacher's Dirty Secret

Feed The Birds

Truth or Dare

The Forbidden Muse

Vigilante

Nightmare Acres

Hallows Fright

Nightmare Acres

ABOUT THE AUTHOR

Dakota is an avid reader, writer, and painter. She lives in the US with her three kids, husband, and their husky. In her free time, she likes to binge watch shows on Netflix with her husband. She also enjoys taking trips with her family to new and exciting destinations.

Want to stay updated on Dakota's upcoming releases? Sign up for her newsletter, or join her Facebook group and become a Hellion.

Head over to www.dakotawildeauthor.com for exclusive merchandise based on Dakota Wilde's books.